Along Comes Scary
ROCK & ROLL NIGHTMARES ·60s EDITION

SHORT STORIES

EDITED BY

STACI LAYNE WILSON

Copyright © 2021 by Staci Layne Wilson

Published by Excessive Nuance in paperback
ISBN-13: 978-1-7375139-0-2

Also available via e-book & audio

OTHER
ROCK & ROLL NIGHTMARES

ALONG COMES SCARY ('60s EDITION)

GORY DAYS ('80s EDITION)

COMING SOON

NONFICTION EDITION

MOVIE EDITION

CONTENTS

Along Comes Scary

Chain, Chain, Chainsaw
Staci Layne Wilson

It's fair to say I'm a natural-born sideman. Middle child, an average student, and while I had one song in the Hot 100, I never came close to the top spot. I'm a good lead guitarist, sure, but I'm more suited to the role of rhythm. I can sing, but backup vocals are more my thing. Not many people notice me, which is okay.

After all, *she's* the star.

Melody and me are a duo, going by the name Distant Relatives. It's just us onstage, sitting side-by-side on wooden stools with our battle-worn Martin D-28s, and one mic to share. We started out last year playing at coffee houses and county fairs, and we were doing okay. But Melody had bigger ideas. To her, folk music is important... but boring. I mean, how many songs can you sing about the 14th Amendment, shell-shocked soldiers, and the last of the great American hobos before you've said it all?

But I digress. I should have been more suspicious when I met Melody. She was too sexy, too beautiful, to be genuinely interested in me. But I fell for it. And now I'm trapped. Let me explain.

...

I was doing a solo gig at the Hug-A-Mug Café in Pigeon Forge, Tennessee. Maybe not the best venue choice for Vietnam War protest anthems, but at least the owner paid me in free coffee (black only; cream and sugar were extra). I almost made it through my anti-gun opus, *G.I. Jerkoff*, but had to stop after the third dead dove hit my guitar right in the sound-hole.

I exited the stage, and heard one pair of hands applauding. The woman was sitting at the coffee bar, and she was the most stunning creature I'd ever seen. She beckoned me, and I went to heel.

"Great playing," she purred, her voice husky yet smooth—like a hit of Maui Wowie followed by a shot of fine cognac. "Can I buy you a coffee?"

"No thanks," I replied, sitting beside her. "I get my drinks for free here."

"Well, how else can I show my appreciation for your performance?"

I didn't know what to say. I started loosening my guitar strings so I could shake out the bloodied bird feathers.

"Marvin!" she snapped her fingers to bring my attention back to her. "Don't you think I'm pretty?"

I stopped my fiddling. "Of course I do." Still, she was coming on way too strong. And how did she know my name? Oh, yeah… it was written on the sign outside. "But it's a woman's personality that turns me on."

"Oh, good. I have several."

"Huh?"

"I mean, onstage. I'm a folk singer, and I'm looking for a sideman. I heard you were good, and you are, so here I am."

"Where did you hear this?" I asked. Not with suspicion, as I should have, but in utter bafflement. Yeah, *The Sounds of Silencers* had hit the aforementioned Hot 100, but it tanked at #99, and then stayed only for a week when people figured out that I hadn't written it as a joke.

She cocked her head and gave me a bemused smile. "I want to audition you."

The next thing I knew, I was buck-naked in the back of her Econoline van trying to dodge the cutting sting of a riding crop. Before that night, I would have assumed S&M stood for speed and marijuana, but I've learned a lot since then. She took pity on me, I guess, because she stopped her whipping and gave me a gentle kiss.

She held my face between her palms and appraised me.

"Beige hair, gray eyes, thin lips. You're entirely unremarkable. But those cheekbones... I could cut myself slapping that face." She chuckled, then her gaze roamed the rest of my body, and apparently there was nothing else noteworthy to comment on. "You don't have a girlfriend, do you?"

"No."

She held her whip up, then unscrewed the handle to reveal a gleaming rapier.

I flattened myself against the shag-carpeted wall panel. "What are you doing? I thought this was an audition."

"Yes, and you passed, my cheeky little virgin. Now hold still while I slit your throat."

"Wait, what?"

"Did I stutter? I need to sacrifice a virgin once a week, or I will cease to exist."

"Good thing I'm not a virgin, then."

She was mystified. "Really?" She took a step back but didn't sheathe her weapon. "But your glasses are as thick as Coke bottles. And you're naked but still wearing white socks and sandals. Also, you closed your show with *Tiptoe Through the Tulips*. You even sang it in Tiny Tim's voice. If that isn't the opposite of sex, I don't know what is."

She had some good points there, but I was telling the truth. "I can prove it," I said. "May I get dressed first?"

Melody nodded and gave me some room.

I pulled on my dungarees and fringed leather vest, then reached for my guitar. I thought about bashing her over the head with it, but there wasn't enough room in the van, and besides, I couldn't afford to destroy my instrument. Being a troubadour was my sole source of income, and I had to support my kids.

That's right: I'm not only devirginized, but am also the proud papa of who knows how many tour babies. I may not look like much, but a guy with a guitar—even an acoustic— can still get a lot of tail. I turned my Martin upside-down and gave it a shake. After a few feathers flew free, so did my many paternity suits and Family Court summons.

Melody unfolded and read every one of them. "Wow," she marveled. "You must really need a lot of bread. I wasn't lying when I said I was looking for a second fiddle—er, guitar. I can pay you half my gig fee, and for every virgin you bring me, I'll let you keep whatever's in their wallets."

. . .

So that's how the Distant Relatives' Grand Guignol Hootenanny came about. Now, you might not think airy-fairy folk ballads would mix well with blood-and-guts theatrics, but you'd be wrong. We're a hit everywhere we go.

In fact, I'm a little nervous about the notoriety. But we stick to the big cities, where people are less likely to be missed. Then again, in the big cities, virgins are harder to find. Free love and the Pill are two of Melody's least favorite things. For obvious reasons, of course. But the S&M thing aside, would you believe she's an old-fashioned girl? She's got to be at least 300 years old, so I guess I can't blame her for being a little square.

Our first several gigs were uneventful. I was enjoying myself—I never liked being a solo performer because it's harder to blend in when you're the only one under the spotlight—but then she got bored. Slitting gizzards, slashing throats, and bashing brains after the gigs was leaving her cold. She wanted more.

"There has to be more to death than this," she complained one night, shortly after drinking the blood of a Singing Nun fan who'd wandered into our show by mistake.

"I suppose," I agreed, going through the wallet of the donor. There was a rosary and enough money to fill our tank to the next city, but that was about it. "We need to attract a more upscale clientele."

"Maybe folk music isn't the way to go. Hippies are poor."

As I contemplated how to dispose of the corpse—always the hardest part of my job—an idea came to me. "What about doing a musical? Have you seen the box office numbers for *Hair*? It's on Broadway now, and people, *rich people*, are flocking to see naked dongs onstage."

Melody was brushing her teeth, but she muttered something about modesty and decorum and how she'd never pose nude, not even if Bob Guccione begged her on bended knee. She spit into the sink, then said, "And, no offense, Marvin, but I don't think your dong is going to raise our ticket prices."

I wasn't offended. She was right.

"I've got it!" she shouted so loudly I was afraid the people next door would hear. Normally, we didn't murder music lovers in seedy motels with paper-thin walls, but the van was in the shop.

"It can't be anemia," I replied, whispering to set an example. "What do you got?"

Melody's eyes sparkled. "An idea. A great idea. When I was living in Paris a few decades ago, I went to the *Le Théâtre du*

Grand-Guignol in the Pigalle district. Have you heard of it?"

I shook my head. "I don't even know how to pronounce it. What is it?"

"Grand Guignol theater. In these stage plays, the most horrific and grisliest of deaths are acted out for the titillation and amusement of a bloodthirsty, *paying* audience. It's all fake, of course. But ours won't be." She brought her hands together like a delighted child. "What fun!"

It took us a few weeks to work out the kinks, but now we've got it down. The questionnaire we pass out beforehand is very helpful.

1. Are you over 18?
2. Are you squeamish?
3. Do you understand that photography and audio recording are strictly prohibited?
4. For those in the front row: Would you like to rent a plastic poncho?
5. Are you a Folkie, a Mod, a Rocker, or a member of the Chess Club?
6. Would you like to be a victim in our interactive third act?
7. If you answered yes to Question 6: Are you a virgin?

...

No two performances are exactly the same, of course, but we always go through our acoustic set first, starting with *The Sounds of Silencers*, followed by our joint compositions *War Sucks*, *Circling the Bowl*, and *Arlo Guthrie Stole My Keys*.

Playing music with Melody is like no other experience I can describe. Her androgynous Billie-Holiday-on-acid-voice coupled with the spiraling, cascading strings on her guitar going from 4/4 to 3/4 still gives me chills every time I hear it. I guess that's what makes me stay with her—that and the fact she'd skin me alive if I ever tried to leave.

We end the musical performance portion of our Grand Guignol Hootenanny with my cover of *Tiptoe Through the Tulips*. It has the same effect as it used to—people getting up to leave—but there's a twist.

The theater personnel lock the doors.

Once the audience is captive, and before I get to my final tulip trill, Melody pulls a weapon from her brassier (I told you she's old-fashioned). We generally alternate between switchblades, small pistols, icepicks, and the like.

But tonight, she has stashed a chainsaw behind her stool.

With more discreet weapons, it's easy to pull off the illusion. Melody is an old pro when it comes to slaughtering her victims, so she can subdue and quiet them quickly but still show maximum bloodshed to the audience. We close the curtain while the volunteer is clearly alive, then we unlock the doors. Once the audience has left and Melody's meal is taken to the van, well... that's that.

So far, we've been lucky. I guess I should say *I've* been lucky. I'm the mortal one, and even though I don't use my real name anymore, all this is bound to catch up with me.

Tonight, I feel trapped. She's being far too reckless with my fate.

I'm strumming and singing, but one eye is on Melody as she moves her long peasant skirt aside to reveal the yellow-handled chainsaw propped up against the wooden perch. The audience applauds. She stands, then gestures to our pre-selected third-act volunteer. He's a nebbish fellow, wearing glasses thicker than mine, plus a pocket-protector, a short plaid tie, high-waisted slacks, and monk strap shoes.

I really don't see how we can get away with this. I decide to take matters—and the chainsaw—into my own hands. I toss my Martin aside and swoop down to pick up the power tool.

I fumble with it, not quite sure how to start the thing, but Melody is stunned, and just watches me. Maybe she thinks I'm going to do the honors on tonight's victim? I pull the starter rope three times before the machine roars to life. I hold the chainsaw above my head, then swing it toward Melody. I see the realization in her eyes.

Then she smiles.

Uh-oh. She's not afraid.

The saw buzzes and roars, and above the din I hear the virgin say, "Um, do you still need me?" I swing the chainsaw at him, and he shuffles away so fast he trips on the stage stairs and falls.

In that moment of inattention, Melody tackles me.

My arms sway with the jolt and the chainsaw is heavy, but I don't let it go. The audience applauds and cheers. Those in the front row gather their plastic ponchos up to their chins. I pull myself free, then swoop down, swinging at Melody's skull.

She dodges me, but loses a hand in the process.

It flies through the air like it's waving goodbye.

Melody stares at the bloody stump. "You bastard! How am I going to play guitar now?"

The audience laughs.

My heart pounds. I want to drop the chainsaw and run, but I must see this through now. I raise the weapon again and before Melody can react, I take off her arm at the shoulder.

Great arcs of red soak the audience, who look confused, as if they hadn't expected the fake blood to be so warm and pungent. But they see that Melody is still standing, so they clap.

Melody rushes me with a head-butt to the chest. I respond by taking off her other arm. She responds by kicking me. The chainsaw sputters, but I rev it up and it roars back to life, bits of flesh and bone soaring from its kickback zone.

"I'll just learn to play with my toes!" she snaps.

The audience whoops.

I bring the chainsaw down and across, cutting her off at the knees.

She glowers up at me, clearly furious. I can't say I blame her.

"No problem," she gurgles, balancing on her nubs, "I'll pick with my teeth. If Jimi Hendrix can do it, so can I! You can't stop me!"

I look at the audience. They begin clapping in rhythm, then someone starts a chant: "Do it... do it... do it..."

But I can't.

Melody is harmless now.

...And maybe "Mini Mel" is onto something: a Tiny Tim tribute act featuring a stump who strums a guitar with her teeth could sell a lot of tickets.

Hell-A Woman
Marco Mannone

There might be worse fates than waking up with a hangover only to find yourself tied to a bed as some kind of human sacrifice, but at the moment Lenny Conway couldn't think of one.

He couldn't think of a lot of things, actually. For example, he had difficulty remembering who he was, where he was or how he got there... It was night, evident by a window's drapes undulating in a warm breeze. The sounds of a raucous party throbbed its way through the walls of what Lenny could only vaguely recall as... a hotel? While it wasn't entirely unusual for him to wake up in strange places, never before had his hands and feet been bound to a bed frame, clad only in his briefs and suede Chelsea boots.

At first Lenny thought it was a sex thing, and for an all-too-brief moment he considered himself lucky (it had been a while), but the Satanic sigils splattered across the walls in blood made him reconsider.

The blood was on him too, it turned out, crisscrossing the entire king-sized mattress like a crimson target. Burning candles cast strange shadows on everything and illuminated the busy lines of ants that were beginning to trace the bloody patterns in the room. Soon enough they would be crawling on Lenny and infesting his mustache.

He struggled to free himself, causing his beer belly to shimmy like a bowl of pale Jell-O, but the effort caused a surge of pain in his head, ringing the bell of his hangover. Lenny wasn't going anywhere. He looked out the window at what appeared to be snowflakes fluttering across a glowing void.

Los Angeles, he remembered. It can't be snowing in Los Angeles. And that's when it all started to come back to him... the wildfire consuming hundreds of acres to the north, throwing plumes of ash into the atmosphere that were now transforming the Sunset Strip into a surreal winter scene in June.

It's June, Lenny remembered... 1969... and before the strike of midnight, he was going to have his heart cut out by a reclusive rock star in an effort to save her doomed soul.

Lenny Conway could really use a drink.

...

There was a certain sad symmetry to how Lenny woke up that morning: disoriented and in need of a deep-tissue brain massage.

He rolled over in bed and strained to close the blinds that were assaulting him with late morning light. L.A. in the daytime always felt like a bar when they blast the last-call lights: harsh, glaring, exposed—the mystery and romance of night stripped away, revealing a million ugly truths baking in the sun. Which is another way of saying Lenny was not much of a morning person.

A shower beer helped revive him while the coffee brewed.

Feeling somewhat human, Lenny was packing up his reel-to-reel portable tape recorder when the phone rang, sending shockwaves through his skull. It was his *Froth* magazine editor, Barry.

"You up??"

"No, Barry, I'm sound asleep."

"Just checking in. You need anything?"

"Yeah, you getting to your point."

"This interview has cover potential…"

"If I don't fuck it up?"

"Exactly."

Lenny lit a passive aggressive cigarette. "I'm not a suck-up like everyone else. These people are just jerks like the rest of us."

"Not asking you to kiss ass, just try not to rip her a new one."

"I don't even know why I agreed to this. I'm a music critic and Pamela Mercy hasn't made any since that last sorry excuse for an album."

"Think of it more like a human-interest story. What happened to her? Where's she been for the last year? Why all the mystery?"

"If I was interested in humans, I would be writing for *Life*."

"Well, you're writing for me and I'm telling you this is important. Everyone's been wondering what happened to her and she specifically wants *you* to tell her story. God only knows why."

"Life is full of mysteries," Lenny hung up and ashed his cigarette in a dying plant. The walls inched ever so closer to crushing him, or at least whatever spirit he had left. His love affair with L.A. had been curdling for some time and he used the word "insufferable" a lot when describing it to friends who lived elsewhere. But this is where the action was, and as a music critic, he felt obliged to endure it for most of the '60s, which constituted most of his 30s.

But now Lenny was pushing 40 and without much to show for it except a pile of fan letters from juvenile admirers in obscure suburban towns, accumulated during his *Rolling Stone* days. They did little to bolster his self-esteem. The people he really wanted to connect with were the musicians he revered—Brian Jones, Jimi Hendrix, Janis

Joplin, Jim Morrison—but they either dismissed Lenny as a glorified fan or a spiteful hack. As a result, he had to get creative sneaking past club owners who refused him admittance on account of his reputation for being a harsh critic. The accusation never made sense to Lenny, as he signed off every review with "Nothing Personal, LC"—but this cute touch did little to redeem him in the eyes of those he eviscerated in print.

...

A few hours and a couple Tylenol later, Lenny emerged from his ramshackle bungalow on the Venice Canals clutching his recorder case and wearing a "Rock Is Muerto" t-shirt under his thin, chocolate-brown leather jacket—and, of course, sunglasses to mitigate the radioactive ball of fire above. Was he a washed-up rock journalist or an undercover CIA agent slumming it in Havana? By the looks of him you really couldn't tell.

Reflexively, Lenny covered his mouth and nose with a handkerchief to soften the stench of the algae-plagued water. A recent news report on a toxic river in Ohio catching fire made him wary of smoking anywhere near the canals, but his neighbors might not be so discerning. Lenny lived between aging beatniks and young hippies along what was once a fairytale facsimile of Venice, Italy but was now a series of festering irrigation ditches. Back in the day there were twice as many canals that flowed with sparkling vision and promise, but they were eventually paved over to make way for sedans and despair.

On the way to his filthy '58 Plymouth Fury, Lenny passed a young Black fellow lounging on one of the canal bridges wearing an impeccable pinstripe suit and tie, topped off with a tilted fedora. He was focused on tuning his acoustic guitar and paid Lenny no mind. Despite wearing his stylish leather jacket in the escalating heat, a lone chill zigzagged its way through Lenny's core as the man delicately plucked his animal gut strings.

...

The 10 Freeway only affirmed Lenny's disdain for L.A.

The further from the beach he got, the more the atmosphere turned to visible poison—a potent mix of smog and smoke and failed dreams. "SoCal soup," he called it. To his left, Lenny could see plumes rising behind the Hollywood Hills like atomic mushroom clouds. One day they'd be the real deal, he was sure, courtesy of Russia or China.

Lenny turned on the radio (already dialed-in to KABC) and *No Time* by The Guess Who was on—a band he actually didn't mind. "Not bad for a bunch of Canucks," Lenny wrote during his *Rolling Stone* days, before he and Jann had their infamous falling out. The upbeat (yet subtextually ominous) tune moved his mood needle toward Less Cantankerous, but only by a few notches. Traffic was coagulating ahead, as usual, making Lenny reach for his thermos filled with vodka-OJ on ice.

Driving in L.A. forces people to think, whether they like it or not. During commercials, Lenny turned the volume down and was left to ruminate on the impending interview. Pamela Mercy—lead singer of the short-lived, all-female band Angels Outrageous—was for all intents and purposes the next breakout star of this cursed decade, but then poof... she disappeared like a ghost in the night. Rumors abounded, ranging from an alcohol-induced nervous breakdown to being kidnapped by an LSD sex cult. In fact, over the course of her year-long vanishing act, the mystery behind Pamela Mercy overshadowed any of her fleeting musical stardom.

Perhaps most confusing, as Barry pointed out, was why she would reach out to Lenny Conway of all people. *Froth* was barely a rag and he had been particularly brutal towards the Angels' one and only album, *Forever Broken*, to the point he was criticized by other critics for "not having a heart."

Of course, they were wrong. Lenny had a heart—it beat like a fucking war drum against the contrived mediocrity most people mistook for talent.

...

For all his cynicism, Lenny couldn't help but perk up as he cruised the Sunset Strip. This winding, asphalt serpent was still a musical mecca for him, despite its obnoxious popularity. The Sea Witch, Pandora's Box, The Whisky, Le Disc, Hullabaloo, Gazzarri's, The Trip, London Fog... a mile-and-a-half series of ecosystems pulsating with live bands every night from Crescent Heights to Doheny, attracting a whole flood of surging hormones seeking the perfect alchemical arrangement of musical notes and electricity.

There was nothing like it in the world.

Predictably, the whole scene had become a put-on: the hippies and freaks had gone from being a grassroots cultural movement to a slick marketing campaign engineered by the record companies. Everything that starts with magic and soul eventually becomes a parody of itself. It's always been the tragic law of music and probably life itself. Of this, Lenny was certain.

...

"What do you mean I can't park here? I'm a journalist!" Lenny held up his laminated (expired) *Rolling Stone* pass, but the parking attendant for the Chateau Marmont was not impressed.

"Guests only," was all he would say.

"But I was invited here by..." Lenny remembered his instructions from Pamela: they were to use assumed names or the interview was off. Before backing out of the driveway, he flipped off the attendant and referred to him as a "parking fascist."

A few blocks and too many minutes later, Lenny finally found an open spot and fed the ever-hungry meter. The bonfire-scented air momentarily conjured youthful memories of upstate New York summers, but this made him sad so he focused on his surroundings as he walked.

The nightlife action was still hours away and there were already clusters of dazed, barefoot teenagers tripping on god-knows-what, along with the square tourists with neatly-parted hair who took photos of them from afar like they were safari animals.

Lenny didn't do hallucinogens, not after a bad trip he had involving his father burning alive, but he understood the desperate need for escapism. After all, the decade that started with the President's brains being blown out across Dallas like morbid confetti was about to end with America sticking its phallic flag into the moon—no doubt infecting it with our relentless ambition. Throw in some crushed revolutions and an endless bitch of a jungle war and he could see why so many kids would regard the copious consumption of mind-altering substances as the only sane thing left to do. Hemingway jumped the gun before he used it: this was the Lost Generation.

As Lenny approached the hotel entrance, he spotted a young Black fellow playing a sorrowful blues tune across the street... who looked remarkably similar to the guitarist from Venice: wearing the same pinstripe suit and tilted fedora, but it couldn't be. There was no conceivable way he could have beaten Lenny here, except by helicopter.

Once again, a distinct chill navigated its way through Lenny.

...

The Chateau Marmont was a rockstar sanctuary hiding in plain sight, and the last place a music critic the likes of Lenny would typically be welcome—but that didn't stop him from strolling into the lobby like he owned the joint.

"Mr. Jones here for Ms. Cinderella," Lenny informed the sour concierge. "She's expecting me," he added.

The concierge picked up the phone and dialed... "Ms. Cinderella? I'm sorry to bother you but a 'Mr. Jones' is here... Of course." He hung up and gestured across the lobby. "Take the elevator to the 7th floor, Room 79."

Lenny crossed the lobby, purposefully not acknowledging any of the fashionable guests who were draped over the furniture (he didn't want to give them the satisfaction in case they were famous). Like any typical Hollywood celebrity, the French Gothic-style hotel was well-preserved despite its age: constructed in the 1920s, it remained frozen in time with creaky dark wood that ran up the walls and tattered floor runners lining the uneven tile that extended through the lobby and into the maroon-carpeted bar. The whole place, all the way up to the vaulted ceilings, was dimly lit like a museum—or perhaps more accurately—a mausoleum. A very exclusive mausoleum.

Lenny entered the elevator. He didn't like elevators. As gravity pressed down on him, he was confronted by a mirror and felt a dull pang of disgust: he couldn't shake the feeling literary success had officially eluded him. He was born too late for Paris in the '20s and too early for L.A. in the '60s. Everyone was younger, prettier, and happier than he was. Deep down, Lenny hoped the fires would keep spreading until the whole damn city was wiped off the map.

The doors opened, interrupting his self-loathing. He walked down a long, eerily-silent hallway until he came to the very end.

Room 79.

...

Lenny knocked and waited.

The hall lights flickered and compelled him to turn around... at the far end of the hall, standing before the elevator, was the guitarist—he stared at Lenny stone-faced and clutching the instrument by his side. Were the unstable lights creating an illusion, or were the man's shadowy eyes actually hollow sockets?

The door unlocked and opened as far as the security chain would allow, revealing a slice of a fearful eye.

Lenny startled.

"You alone, man?" a girl's raspy voice whispered.

"Who else would I be with?"

The door closed and the chain was unfastened. Lenny glanced over his shoulder but the guitarist was gone. Another (deeper) chill crept through his limbs and this time lingered.

The door opened, revealing Pamela Mercy: a waifish 27-year-old wearing a psychedelic bell sleeve top, shredded denim pants (offering glimpses of feral legs) and no shoes. Her dark hair was an unkempt lioness mane that framed a pale-but-undeniably alluring face beset by troubled eyes.

Lenny instantly resented how attracted he was.

Her brow creased. "You okay, man?"

He nodded and copped a casual attitude. "Ms. Cinderella, I presume?"

"Come in," she said curtly and gestured with her head. The way she closed and locked the door behind Lenny gave him the uneasy impression she was paranoid.

The room (more of an apartment) was also dimly-lit. Candles burned and unseen incense sweetened the air. What should've been a luxurious bohemian hideaway overlooking the entire twinkling sprawl of the city instead felt claustrophobic. Lenny, by no means an empath, couldn't help but notice the vibe was unmistakably weird in here. Heavy.

The wall-to-wall religious artifacts might've had something to do with it. Solemn crucifixes, palm-shaped hamsas, Buddhist wheels of life, Sanskrit—and scores of other esoteric symbols of indeterminate origin— covered nearly every vertical surface. Some were dusty relics while others were scribbled directly onto the walls in what looked to be a frenzy.

Pills, Lenny thought. He'd known people— —roadies, groupies, and a few editors at *Rolling Stone*—who'd had made the mistake of popping. Booze takes its eventual toll, but pills will waste no time twisting a decent person into a balloon animal made by a baby-eating circus clown.

"Can I fix you a drink?" Pamela asked, sounding slightly more at ease. "Got a full bar."

Lenny gingerly laid his recorder case on the coffee table and set it up. "Vodka on the rocks with a squeeze of lemon or lime would hit the spot."

While she made his libation, Lenny couldn't help but notice an airline ticket among the clusters of abandoned takeout boxes and tarot cards that littered the table: LAX to Mexico City. Dated the very next day. He thought nothing of it at the time as there were still more peculiar details to distract him... such as the piles of ancient-looking books stuffed with brittle pages.

Pamela handed him his drink. "Bottoms up, partner."

"Thanks. Do we need to wait for someone?" he asked with his finger poised over the record button.

"Nope." She lit a joint with a white disposable lighter, her hands trembling almost imperceptibly.

Lenny pressed record and the reels started spinning. "So, Pamela. Why am I here?"

She took a long toke and leaned by the open window with a crossed arm, gazing upon the concept of L.A. "I have a story to tell."

"No, why am *I* here? I wasn't very, how should we say, gracious toward your album."

"Shit, man. I've got thicker skin than that," Pamela scoffed, but it actually made her cry at the time. "Truth be told, I need someone like you to tell my story. You can't help but vomit the truth, can you? No matter how messy it gets."

"My truth, sure. But I didn't just fight crosstown traffic to talk about me..."

A long pause ensued as she continued to look out the window. "Do you believe in evil?"

"I think Nixon is proof enough."

Pamela spun around. "Screw Tricky Dick, man! I'm talking about actual *evil* evil. The kind that contaminates your very soul."

"Well toward the end there, working at *Rolling Stone* kinda felt like that."

Pamela stubbed the joint out in an ashtray with contempt. "You can joke all you want but you won't be laughing when I tell you my truth."

Lenny took a sip of his vodka, "I'm listening..."

...

Pacific Palisades, 1967

Pamela didn't mean to join a cult, but these things had a way of happening in California at that time. And while it wasn't an "LSD sex cult" per se, there was a lot of both. But that wasn't the point. It was all about deprogramming themselves from the hypocritical/corrupt capitalist social construct they were subjected to since birth (it just so happened that doing so involved a lot of tripping and fucking). For Pamela, specifically, it was a rebellious means to a creative end. After spending years struggling to make a name for herself as a singer, she felt it was time for something bold.

And "bold" was one adjective people used to describe Charlie the night Pamela met him at Brian Wilson's party. She was invited to a lot of music industry soirées—courtesy of her movie producer father—but most of them bored her to tears.

This one was different.

All night long Charlie had been courting, or was courted by, a slew of braless young things with feathers and flowers decorating their unwashed hair like nubile Christmas trees. Objectively speaking, Charlie wasn't much to look at—diminutive and disheveled as he was—yet he was like a charismatic storm front: wherever he swirled, the pressure and energy changed instantly without even uttering a word. To exemplify this, one of his girls blindfolded herself and sat in the middle of the bustling party waiting for Charlie to enter. When he finally appeared at the other end of the loud room, the girl smiled and squealed, "There he is!" It was an uncanny party trick to say the least, but also an effective one.

So when Charlie ended up giving Pamela his undivided attention in Wilson's expansive backyard, she felt privileged. "Everyone needs to shed their snake skin," he told her while they shared a joint overlooking moonlit bluffs. "The System doesn't want us to evolve, it wants us to stay slithering around the

Garden of Eden like we are. But this is our garden, dig? And we need to shed what we are in order to inherit what we deserve."

The Biblical analogy resonated with a change-starved Pamela. As it turned out, Charlie was also an aspiring musician, but his ambitions transcended mere fame and fortune. As Pamela became ingratiated with his "family"—over the course of a dreamy summer that started with jam sessions on the beach and ended with hallucinogenic mountain orgies—she learned his sights were set on "grand scale spiritual initiation." In order to help them achieve this, whatever it meant, Charlie said they needed a little help from the Other Side.

So, one evening, they packed into their refurbished (stolen) school bus and headed up to Death Valley to perform an invocation that would bring about "the end of the '60s and the world as we know it." During the four-hour drive into the high Martian desert, Charlie explained there was an entity known as "Clauneck" that could help them manifest their wildest dreams. According to him, the cancerous spread of Christianity over the ages was an effort to suppress alternative deities that could empower their worshippers.

"These ancient rituals have been buried by the sands of time, that is, until now." Charlie produced an antique-looking brass oil lamp adorned with intricate Islamic engravings. "Check this shit out..." He held it up and the way it reflected the moonlight seemed unnatural to Pamela. Then again, her veins were usually coursing with something unnatural. She was compelled to touch it, which Charlie allowed. The moment her fingers came in contact with the cold metal her whole body tingled with a confusing blend of intense arousal and overwhelming dread.

"What's inside?" she asked in a reverent whisper.

Charlie grinned. "I'll show you."

How Charlie came into possession of such a strange item was open to debate. He claimed he scored it at a pawn shop but... rumor has it there was a professor of anthropology up in Berkeley who had his face pulverized by a hammer during a late-night home invasion in which several rare antiquities were reported missing. That Charlie was in the Berkeley area at the time of this brutal homicide was purely circumstantial, but once news broke, his girls noticed he was mighty anxious to head south down the coast.

Regardless of how he obtained the unique artifact, it was his now and trips to the library had convinced him it contained dark powers that could be conjured at will—providing one supplied exactly 27 drops of sacrificial blood under a full moon. Which is why Charlie and his girls ended up at Barker Ranch at the base of the Panamint mountains. As they filed out into the frigid night, they were met with a chorus of howling coyotes—no doubt celebrating a fresh kill. Charlie took this as a good omen. Above them, the entire universe was on display and looking up at it made Pamela feel like a shrinking molecule.

"Unload the wood and start a fire," Charlie commanded as he sauntered off toward a dilapidated barn. The property belonged to one of the girl's grandparents, who owned a small mining company and resided on an adjacent ranch about half a mile down the dirt road. Barker is where they kept their machinery and some livestock, which made it the ideal setting for what Charlie and his girls were about to do. He selected a robust hog (symbolizing prosperity) and tied a rope around its neck before leading the docile swine to the growing bonfire. Charlie then fastened it to a dead tree before locking eyes with Pamela. "Newbie," he barked as he unsheathed a massive hunting knife. "Will you do the honors?"

Pamela's gut contracted. She was a devout animal lover her whole life and a strict vegetarian since high school, but was now being tasked with slaughtering this innocent creature.

"Don't think nothing of it," Charlie reassured. "His blood wants to come out."

The girls stared at Pamela with flaming pupils.

"What do I do?" she asked timidly. Charlie answered by running a finger across her throat and placing the knife in her hand. Pamela nodded and walked over to the hog... but hesitated. The girls egged her on: "Do it!" "Slice that fucker open!" "Death to the pig!"

Pamela frowned and imagined the hog was every executive who rejected her music but wanted her pussy... She plunged the blade into the swine's jugular in such a way that blood sprayed everywhere—onto her, Charlie, the girls, and the burning logs with a brief sizzle.

Pamela's scream was a combination of horror and triumph and the girls joined her.

Charlie sprang to action and used an eye dropper to collect the blood draining from the dead hog. He then placed the antique oil lamp on the ground and delicately squeezed the aforementioned 27 drops into its spout. "In the Book of Genesis, God creates humans in the 27th verse. In Kabbalah, the 27th path is where the nature of everything found in the orb of the sun is perfected. In Buddhism, 27 is the highest level of spiritual attainment in the material world…"

One of the girls handed Charlie an ancient-looking book, which he opened with the enthusiasm of a teenager opening *Playboy*. He began reading aloud in some unknown dialect as the bonfire intensified and a gust of wind kicked up cyclones of dirt along with their billowing hair.

Pamela could taste the bitter hog's blood on her chapped lips as she looked on in disbelief: the girls were dancing like possessed Greek nymphs in a dust storm while Charlie shouted in bizarre tongues, all the while the glittering cosmos above went dark, one doomed galaxy at a time… until the sky was nothing but a black abyss.

The fire blew out, plunging them into a world of shadows, yet the brass oil lamp somehow kept reflecting its flames. It then became the epicenter of an earthquake as cracks shot through the ground in all directions, making the entranced girls stumble into each other's arms. From the lamp's spout emerged a black cloud, out of which arose a tall entity that loomed over them with its long arms spread open: Clauneck.

The wind stopped blowing and the dust settled, allowing Clauneck to be seen in all of its grotesque glory, like something out of a Hieronymus Bosch painting: it was a gaunt, elderly figure with horns of varying sizes protruding from its hunchback. In contrast, it bore a jarringly attractive, genderless face that anyone could fall in love with. Perhaps most notably, it also exhibited both male and female genitalia, each visibly eager for some kind of ungodly procreation.

Charlie threw his arms open with demented joy. "Far, fucking, OUT!"

Clauneck responded by rearing its angelic face inches from his own... and opening its mouth, revealing a quivering gullet lined with rows of fangs. It released a sound best described as the collective suffering of every living creature that ever existed.

By the time Charlie's girls screamed, he was already running back to the school bus as fast as he could. If Charlie really wanted to bring about the end of the '60s and the world as we know it, he would simply have to find another way.

The girls quickly joined him, but not Pamela. Sure, she was terrified, but also resolved to understand what Charlie meant when he said Clauneck could "make their wildest dreams come true." Pamela soon realized the hermaphroditic entity could communicate telepathically—not with words, but feelings and visuals. Clauneck wasn't going to hurt her. It was going to serve her. It knelt before Pamela—its bony joints cracking along the way—and asked what she wanted more than anything. Before she could formulate an answer, at least verbally, a beam of light sucked her up into the abyss...

... And gently deposited her on a stage in front of 10,000 screaming fans. As Pamela leaned into a microphone, her audience fell silent, hanging on her every word... "I want to be a rock star." The crowd erupted in cheers, camera bulbs exploded, and Pamela Mercy became awash in a warm sensation she could only decipher as unconditional love.

It was the first time she ever felt it.

Pamela closed her teary eyes and dove into the crowd, which promptly consumed and digested her.

She awoke the next day caked in dirt and blood, and smiling from ear to ear. Charlie and the girls abandoned Pamela but she didn't care. She knew in her bones, down to her very marrow, she was destined for greatness.

Her feeling was vindicated when, while hitchhiking back to L.A. along the 178, she was picked up by a roaring Shelby Cobra Daytona Coupe (one of only six ever made). Behind the wheel was a nebbish young man with mutton chops who gawked at her ruined appearance. "Hot damn, you okay?"

Pamela leaned through the passenger window, allowing her cleavage to work its magic. "Some parties are crazier than others. If I promise not to get your seat dirty, you think you could give me a ride to L.A.?"

"Darling, you can dirty anything you want..." He leaned over and opened the door for her.

Pamela sat down and closed it. "You look awfully familiar, partner. Where do I know you from?"

He offered his hand and she shook it. "Name's Spector," he said with a crooked smile. "Phil Spector."

The serendipity of being picked up in the middle of nowhere by one of the most influential record producers in the music industry was not lost on Pamela. This was more than serendipity. This was destiny. As it happened, he got turned around in a dust storm and was totally lost when he came upon her on the side of the road. They hit it off immediately and by the time they were speeding through Lancaster he had agreed to help her form a band.

Pamela licked the crusty hog blood from her lips once more... but this time it tasted sweet.

...

Lenny swallowed the last of his vodka. It was putting his hangover in its place, thank Christ, but this didn't make him feel any better about interviewing a delusional young woman who obviously needed clinical help. "Sounds like you had a bad trip." He suppressed a burp. "Happens to the best of us."

"This was no trip, man!" she retorted. "This shit happened."

"So you attribute your brief success to... a genie out of Aladdin's lamp?"

"Not a genie. A jinn demon. And yes, that's what I'm telling you. I mean, everything started to fall into place after that night: I hooked up with the biggest producer in the biz, formed a band, recorded an album, and before I knew it, we were opening for The Stones, The Doors, Hendrix, Janis. All within the span of a year."

"Girls like you tend to get lucky. It ain't exactly mystical."

"Girls like me? What's that supposed to mean?"

"You're a Topanga Canyon princess with a Hollywood daddy. Plus, you're easy on the eyes. Just a matter of time before someone who mattered noticed."

Pamela did her best not to sound indignant. "Sure, man. I suppose you're right. My father opened some doors for me. But all walking through them ever did was have married men try to fuck me in their corner offices while my demos played."

Lenny sighed, "Look. I came here to get the scoop on why a rising rock star ditched her band just when she was about to start headlining. What's any of this hocus-pocus crap have to do with why you've been M.I.A.? Have you been hiding from this Charlie character? Is that why you asked if I was alone?"

"His love letters started sounding more like death threats while I was on the road, but Charlie's the least of my worries right now. Just when things were going good, that's when the dreams started. First when I was asleep... but now even when I'm awake."

Lenny's head fell back on the sofa, already regretting his next question: "What kind of dreams?"

"I'm being visited... haunted... by a Black cat. A blues musician. He's been trying to warn me for the past year."

This description got Lenny's attention, but he maintained a poker face. "Warn you about what?"

"My fate. You see, Clauneck's wishes come with a catch: it will grant you whatever you want, but you have to pay up when you're 27, and the price is your soul."

"Great. So I'm too old to sell my soul even if I wanted to?" Lenny asked sardonically.

Pamela shrugged. "I didn't make the rules, man."

"How old are you again?"

"Twenty-seven."

"And when's your birthday?"

Pamela glanced up at a clock with palpable dread. It was quarter to nine. She headed to the bar and poured herself a Southern Comfort on the rocks. "In about three hours," she answered before draining her whiskey in one committed gulp.

"So, you quit the band and holed up in here until you could find a way to save your soul? In a nutshell?"

Pamela nodded. "Touring is murder. Just ask Buddy Holly and the rest of those poor bastards. Nuh-uh. No planes, no hard drugs, nothing. I've been laying low and reading up on demons and curses like a good girl."

Lenny needed her to come to her senses if for no other reason than he was starting to absorb her paranoia through osmosis. "No one's haunting you. They're just dreams. Any shrink can tell you that."

"I wish..." Pamela leafed through one of the ancient-looking volumes she had laying around and pulled an old photo she was using as a bookmark. "The song he keeps playing whenever he shows up. Took me a while but

I knew I knew it: *Cross Road Blues*. This isn't just any bluesman I've been seeing. This is Robert Johnson..." She handed the photo to Lenny and he shuddered: it was the very same guitarist he had been seeing all day.

"Robert Johnson," Pamela continued in a campfire tone, "was rumored to have sold his soul to the Devil in Mississippi in order to become a better musician. And it worked. For about two years. Then he died in 1938 under mysterious circumstances... at the age of 27."

Lenny's stomach turned to ice. "Even if I believed you, printing this conversation would only make things worse. It's a little hard to make music in a straightjacket."

Pamela took the photo back and her face hardened. "I lived my dream, short as it was. Now I wanna live my life. And the only way I can do that is by making a sacrificial offering. A soul in place of my own."

"Another pig?"

"Kinda," she answered coldly.

Lenny started to feel detached from his body... like he was drowning inside of it, unable to reach himself.

"Something wrong?" Pamela inquired.

"I could use some air..." He stood up and nearly lost his balance.

She helped steady him, "Easy now."

"I'm not usually as much of a lightweight as this," Lenny slurred as he made concentrated steps toward the veranda. He weaved involuntarily, knocking over a lamp.

"It's not your fault. I made a hell of a cocktail," Pamela teased while dropping the needle on Nancy Sinatra's *Boots* album—specifically, the dramatic ballad, *In My Room*.

"I'm good," Lenny mumbled before collapsing to the floor in an awkward position. He strained to move but the effort made him piss his pants. All he could do was moan in shame.

Pamela removed the spools from his recorder and ripped the tape out while blissfully swaying to the music.

Fucking Geminis, was Lenny's last thought before passing out.

...

Lenny stirred awake tied to the bed in his underwear and boots.

Candles illuminated bloody, Satanic sigils defacing the walls and bed (and crawling with ants).

There was no sign of Pamela.

Although he was never good at them, Lenny was finely attuned to the algorithm of parties. By the pitch and volume of the bacchanal pulsing its way through the walls, he estimated a couple hours must've passed since Pamela slipped him the mickey.

"HEY! SOMEONE HELP ME!" he shouted but all it did was make his head pound (the chloral hydrate encouraged his hangover to return with a vengeance). He struggled to loosen his binds but Pamela must've been a fucking Girl Scout when she was little because they were not budging.

"The Angels lack any shred of musical ability," Pamela appeared from the flickering shadows, casually brandishing a rather large dagger. "Unable to harmonize, they sing in unison like a bunch of whiny, out-of-tune schoolgirls from another dimension—which probably makes them sound way hipper than they could ever hope to be."

It took Lenny a moment to realize she was quoting his review of her album, "You memorized it?"

She continued, "*Forever Broken* is the creative abortion of a group of girls who would be better suited as groupies. This is the epitome of disposable music, the likes of which—if there is a God—will be *Forever Forgotten* soon enough... So tell me, Lenny. Is there a God?"

"Pamela, please! They're just words!"

She dragged the tip of the dagger across Lenny's soft belly—the slightest amount of pressure would puncture it. "Words can cut deep," she pouted.

"I'm sorry, okay? I was jealous!"

"Jealous? Of me?"

"Of all of you! Everyone who got to play their music and make albums and go on tours. I wanted to be in a band. I was in a band. Back in college. We were good, too. But me and the singer fell for the same chick and she went with him and I quit. So you see? I'm just another asshole who couldn't hack it."

"I appreciate your honesty but that doesn't change the fact a jinn demon is coming for my soul."

"That Charlie guy really did a number on you. If you drop enough acid with the wrong people, you'll believe all kinds of crazy shit. Untie me and I'll help you straighten out…"

Pamela raised the dagger above her head, "Sorry, partner. But it's almost midnight and a soul is going to Hell one way or another…"

"Wait! Uh… Perfect people and their perfect things / Cold puppets on their lonely strings / The stage is set, the lights are on / But no one claps, when there is no song…"

Pamela froze. "You know my lyrics?"

"You wrote some good stuff! Really. I didn't want to admit it at the time. I honestly figured nothing I could say would stop you from becoming the next big thing. I was just venting. Can you forgive me??"

Pamela's eyes were wet and scornful. "I don't think the world will cry over one less critic... Nothing personal."

Lenny shut his eyes. The irony was not lost on him: he barely aged out of the draft just in time to avoid getting blown-up in Vietnam and now he was about to die in a luxury hotel on the Sunset Strip. Neither were preferable.

Pamela plunged the dagger down... but inches before it could pierce Lenny's heart, a clawed, bony hand grabbed her arm... belonging to Clauneck. Pamela recoiled but the demon's grip was vice-like. She gestured to Lenny with her free hand and pleaded, "Wait! I have a soul for you! He's all yours!"

Clauneck turned to Lenny, narrowing its almost-human eyes, and watched as he squirmed on the bloodstained mattress having a total freak-out. The demon turned back to Pamela and shook its head. *A deal's a deal. Time to die.*

Pamela snatched the dagger with her free hand and stabbed Clauneck's chest. The demon pulled the blade out and discarded it, making an inky fluid gush down its wrinkled torso. It wiped some off with its index claw and used its other hand to pin a crying Pamela to the wall by her arm.

"NO! PLEASE! I WANNA LIVE!" she begged and kicked in vain.

Lenny watched in terror as Clauneck used its dripping claw to inject Pamela's arm. It then released her, letting her stagger for the door… but her breathing became labored as she fell to her knees. The demon's blood was coursing through Pamela, causing her body to violently convulse on the floor in teeth-cracking agony. Her last sound was a pathetic gurgle as her eyes rolled back and her limbs stopped spasming.

Pamela Mercy was dead, just minutes before her 28th birthday.

"Jesus Christ, Jesus Christ…" Lenny kept whimpering.

Clauneck approached him with a nightmare for a smile and used its claws to slash his binds, freeing him. He cowered helplessly before the demon lifted him up by his throat and hoisted him outside the open window—seven stories above West Hollywood. There was nothing but a scream between Lenny and the pavement, but at the moment, Clauneck's stranglehold prevented him from making a sound.

The demon got in Lenny's head and told him he was too old for consumption—a dull, bitter spirit. Clauneck's delicacy of choice were those who burned bright in this world, and who burned brighter than young rock stars? They were the caviar of souls and now the demon was free to feast on them once more. Lenny, on the other hand, would go on to live a long, miserable life before dying alone. When he was gone, there would be no one to mourn him and no music to carry on his legacy—the ultimate death.

Clauneck released Lenny.

He flailed through the air as the sidewalk rushed toward him...

...but Lenny landed on the floor of the bedroom next to Pamela's body.

The demon was gone.

...

Lenny emerged from Room 79 in a cold sweat. Clothed and clutching his recorder case, he headed for the elevator at the end of the hall. If he could just make it back down to the street, maybe his sanity wouldn't completely unravel.

He pressed the button and looked over his shoulder, expecting to see something horrible, but the hall behind him was empty.

The elevator doors opened, revealing a scrappy, bearded man with shoulder-length hair and fierce eyes. He wore a fringed Davy Crockett jacket and a perverted grin. "Peace and blessings, brother," the man said as he flashed the peace sign.

"Excuse me," Lenny muttered as they squeezed past each other, switching places.

He pressed the button for the first floor and the doors were almost shut... when the man's arm burst inside and pried them open.

Although the man was grinning, his voice simmered with danger. "Say brother, maybe you can help me. I'm lookin' for a friend of mine. I know she's on this floor, just not sure which room. Goes by Pamela or Newbie."

Lenny realized he was face-to-face with Charlie, and had he been paying attention when he entered the hotel earlier, he would've recognized him as one of the hippies hanging in the lobby.

Lenny cleared his throat and replied, "Nope. Sorry."

Charlie's grin faded, and that's when Lenny noticed the handle of a .38 snub-nosed revolver sticking out of his denim pants. "Don't lie to me, brother. I can always tell when people lie to me."

After being suspended out of a window by a hermaphroditic demon, Lenny was in no mood to be threatened by anyone wearing fringe, even if they were packing. "You wanna know the truth?" he said with his own hint of danger. "You'll find her body getting cold on the floor of room 79. She was poisoned by Clauneck, who's now free to prey on bright souls, thanks to you."

Charlie had not anticipated hearing any of this and was, for the first and only time in his life, at a complete loss for words.

Lenny was prepared for violence, evident by his free hand discreetly balling into a white-knuckled fist.

Instead, Charlie crossed his eyes and darted his tongue like a lizard... before letting the doors close.

Lenny's fist remained clenched all the way down to the lobby.

...

He exited the Chateau Marmont as nonchalantly as possible. The whole Strip faded from view in a shroud of smoke under an unnaturally orange sky, like a neon interpretation of Dante's Inferno. Of course, the apocalyptic atmosphere did little to deter the hordes of teenagers from *carpe noctis*. Ashes continued to float down like snow as Lenny pushed through them in a shell-shocked daze. There may have still been six months left in this godforsaken decade, but for Lenny, the '60s—or at least the naive idealism part of it stood for—ended that very night.

Seeing his filthy '58 Plymouth Fury was like seeing land after being lost at sea— parking ticket be damned. Lenny got inside, locked the doors, and lit a cigarette with shaky hands. He savored the first drag and the fractured shards of his mind started to mend... Maybe Pamela spiked his drink with more than chloral hydrate. She was an acid head, after all, and what was more probable: that Lenny just witnessed a supernatural murder, or that he hallucinated exactly what she had described to him in her story? The coroner would no doubt list her cause of death as an overdose, most likely from heroin. And since they used fake names, there was no record of him ever actually being there (save for the concierge, who would have no real way of ID'ing Lenny) so he wouldn't be implicated one way or another.

Drugs, he thought. *An entire generation is about to have a major comedown soon enough.*

Lenny turned the key and his engine rumbled to life, along with the radio. It took a moment for him to recognize the old song... *Cross Road Blues* by none other than Robert Johnson. Spooked, he turned the radio off with an all-too-familiar icy sensation creeping through him.

Lenny Conway drove back to Venice in silence.

...

A few weeks later, Brian Jones was found dead at the bottom of his swimming pool in England.

In September of 1970, Jimi Hendrix was found dead covered in his own vomit, also in England.

The following month, Janis Joplin was found dead on the floor of her Hollywood hotel room.

In July of the following year, Jim Morrison was found dead in his Paris bathtub (and on the exact same date as Brian Jones).

Years later, Kurt Cobain and Amy Winehouse would join them.

They were all 27.

Papa's Got a Brand-New Body Bag
Staci Layne Wilson

Malachi never thought growing up in a funeral parlor was cool—until now. *Now* there was a semi-famous rock star lying dead in the basement morgue.

He was upstairs in his sister's bedroom, going through her record collection to see if he could find any Barry Birdsong albums, or even a single, when the phone rang. It was too late to get the rocker to sign it, of course, but maybe Mal could get a fingerprint or something like that. He'd have to be careful, though. His dad, Mortimer (aka Morty the Mortician), would most definitely not approve.

Mal went into the hallway and picked up the phone. "Hackman Funeral Home."

"Man, is it true? You've got Barry Birdsong there?" It was Mal's friend from down the street, Jonas Sharp.

"Um, yeah. But it's supposed to be a secret. His manager is coming to get the body tomorrow, and after that, I guess he'll alert the media. Dad just embalmed him, and then Barry's going to be buried wherever he's from." Mal sighed. "How did you hear about it?"

Jonas chuckled. "You know there aren't any secrets in this Podunk town. Besides, my uncle drives the ambulance. He said Barry was D.O.A. after wrapping his Harley around that tree. What a way to go!"

"Yeah, just like Jan and Dean's *Dead Man's Curve*. Splat! Actually, though, he looks pretty good."

"You've seen him?"

"Of course. He's in the cooler."

"Ooh! Can I come see him?"

"I don't think that's a very good idea—"

"—I'll be there tonight. What time do the olds go to bed?"

...

Mal tiptoed down the stairs at exactly 10 PM to let Jonas in on the ground level. The upstairs was the Hackmans' living area; the main floor held the office and files, casket displays, and a small chapel for grieving and memorial services; and the basement was the morgue. Right now, Barry and old Mrs. Schmidt were the only occupants.

"Shhh..." Mal warned as he opened the door.

Jonas, wearing all black, slipped in like a ninja. He was carrying a backpack slung over one shoulder.

"What are you doing?" It was Mal's older sister, Millicent, who was standing on the landing, looking down. She was wearing a long nightgown, and her hair was in curlers with a scarf over it.

"Shhh..." Mal repeated.

Millicent came down the stairs and looked at the boys sternly.

Mal gestured to Jonas. "He just wants to see Barry."

She crossed her arms, then said, "I can't blame him. I want to get another look, too. Wait here while I put on some clothes."

Mal knew it was pointless to argue with a 16-year-old girl, so he nodded. "But hurry."

She dashed quietly up the stairs.

"Is this your first celebrity?" Jonas asked.

"Unless you count that Dear Agnes advice lady from the paper, then yeah." Mal glanced up the stairs, hoping Millicent wouldn't be too long. "Were you a fan?"

Jonas shrugged. "Barry Birdsong was more for chicks. Kinda sappy for me. I like The Kinks."

"Me, too. They're way cooler."

"Who's way cooler?" Millicent joined the boys, dressed in pedal pushers, a sweater, and canvas tennis shoes. The curlers were out, but she hadn't combed her hair.

Mal looked at her sideways. "You look like you're going somewhere. I mean, somewhere else besides the morgue."

Millicent smirked. "Aren't you the astute one, baby brother? Jenny's having a party, and since I'm up and sneaking around anyway, I might as well go. You don't tell on me, and I won't tell on you."

There was always a catch.

"Come on," Jonas prompted, taking a few steps away from the front door. "Is it this way?"

Millicent took three long, fast strides to overtake Jonas, and then she led the way to the basement door.

Mal had been down here countless times throughout his life, but it was always unsettling after hours. He tried not to think about it, especially on sleepless, stormy nights, and he knew his sister felt the same way.

The stairs were steep, and the floral wallpaper that adorned the walls of the rest of the house was left off in the morgue and embalming room—bare cinderblock walls and an unfinished wood-beamed ceiling with bare lightbulbs hanging down was it. The floor was cement, slightly sloped, and it had two large drains in the center to bear blood and other bodily fluids away.

"Whoa, creepy," Jonas noted, third in line down the stairs.

Millicent touched down on the floor, then flicked the light switch, illuminating the small, chilly chamber. They had only six body drawers and three metal embalming tables, but that was usually enough. Morty's tools of the trade were laid out on a rolling table, and his smock hung on a hook on the far side of the room. Several body bags were folded and stacked neatly on a chair.

"Rank," muttered Jonas, wrinkling his nose. The tangy scent of blood and innards clashed with the intense medicinal smell of embalming fluid and bleach.

"You get used to it," Millicent said.

Mal went to the bank of drawers. He touched the handle of the one in the middle. "Welcome to the Gratefully Dead Funeral Home," he said dramatically. "We leave no rock star uninterred." He gave the drawer a pull, revealing the occupant.

Barry Birdsong did look pretty good, considering what he'd been through in the last 12 hours. First, he'd slammed into a giant oak tree going an estimated 80 mph, which crushed his ribcage and burst his heart open. Then, even though he was clearly dead, he'd been hauled to the local hospital for the official pronouncement. After that, he was bagged, tagged, and taken to the funeral home for embalming. All in all, not a great day for would-be the teen idol.

Barry's career was just starting to take off. He'd released two moderately successful albums, made the cover of *Tiger Beat* (in the small square upper-right corner picture, but still), and his latest single, *Why Me?* was slowly but surely climbing the charts. The Confederate-flag-waving crooner, whose lyrics all had a conservationist message, had been on his way to a gig on his "Good Old Boy" tour of small Southern towns when tragedy (and the tree) struck.

"So sad," sighed Millicent. "He was handsome."

Mal was about to cover the corpse back up when a flash of white light momentarily blinded him. "What the—?"

Jonas, who'd been carrying a Polaroid camera in his backpack, was waving the just-ejected print in the air, shaking it for quicker development. "I can't wait to show this around school tomorrow."

"No!" Mal whisper-yelled, lunging forward to snatch the picture away from his friend.

Jonas easily evaded him, and Mal gave up.

Millicent leaned in for a look. "Great shot," she said. Then she gasped. "I have an idea! Why don't we take Barry to Jenny's party?

Wouldn't that be a gas? Her parents are out of town, and everybody's gonna be there."

Mal couldn't believe it. Not that he was being invited, in a roundabout sort of way, to a cool older kid's party, but that his sister could be such an idiot. If they got caught, which they most assuredly would, their dad would kill and embalm them and then their mom'd probably spit on their graves. They took the family business *beyond* serious. Mal looked at his sister incredulously. "Are you insane?"

Millicent was, as usual, ignoring him. "Hey, Jonas," she said with her winning smile, "grab one of those body bags over there. We can go out the exit," she pointed at a nearby door, the one the hearses pulled up to, "then between the three of us, we can carry him to Jenny's. It's only two backyards away if we use the shortcut through the woods."

Mal could see that he was outnumbered, so he helped wedge the cumbersome stiff into a body bag and zipped it closed. They rocked Barry off the gurney, then struggled to hold him as they took slow steps toward the door.

The teens dropped him to the grass once they were outside. Millicent pointed out the route, and they hoisted the unwitting party favor back into the air. She and Jonas each took a corner at Barry's head, and Mal grabbed the feet. The body was heavier than they'd anticipated, but soon they were at Jenny's backdoor and Millicent was turning the knob.

The shindig was in full swing. The Zombies' *She's Not There* was playing on the hi-fi, and high-schoolers were crammed into the kitchen and the den beyond, chatting, dancing, and drinking from Styrofoam cups. Mal could see several bottles of booze on the counter, a large, half-full punch bowl, bags of opened potato chips, cigarette butts overflowing from ashtrays, and even a few joints and roaches. He wondered how Jenny would get rid of the smell before her parents got back, but it wasn't his problem. His problem was keeping an eye on the time— and making sure Barry Birdsong got back to the mortuary in one piece and long before dawn.

As the trio heaved the black body bag into the kitchen, then laid it on the floor, several partygoers gathered around them. Jenny pushed her way to the front.

"Hey, Jen," Millicent said brightly. "I brought a special guest."

Jenny frowned. "Is that a dead body? Gross! Get it out of here."

A chorus of protests rose.

"No!"

"Let's see!"

"Who is it?"

"This party is so dead!"

Millicent knelt, then unzipped the bag slowly, playing into the suspense of the moment.

Barry, his eyes and mouth glued shut but with an otherwise serene countenance, lay there exposed.

Jenny cocked her head. "I don't get it. Who is he?"

"Barry Birdsong!" Jonas announced, spreading his arms wide. "The singer."

"Who let the freshmen in here?" someone at the back of the crowd complained. "They're worse than dead people."

"Mellow," said Millicent, "this is Jonas, and that's my brother, Mal. I needed their help carrying Barry."

Jenny took a step closer and peered down. "Wow. It *is* him. What happened?"

"Motorcycle accident," Mal replied. "But look, we can't stay. We just wanted you to see him. We'd better split now."

Millicent stood and put her hand over Mal's mouth. "Don't listen to the blockhead." She looked at the crowd. "Come on, help me get him into the living room. We can put him on the couch."

Most everyone was too squeamish to touch the nude cadaver, but a few particularly drunk and stoned senior boys eventually stepped up. Mal began to sweat as he watched them propping Barry up on the sofa, then crossing his legs as if he was just there hanging out.

Jonas brandished his camera and said, "Hey, Jenny and Millicent, why don't you sit next to him? I'll take a picture!"

The girls laughed, then obliged. Jenny took a cigarette from one of the nearby ashtrays and tried to jam it into Barry's mouth without much success.

"His lips are glued shut," Millicent explained.

Jenny's eyes went to Barry's johnson. "Why is it so shriveled?"

"I guess because he's been drained of all his blood. That is kind of gross, though." Millicent grabbed an ivory lace doily from the couch arm and dropped it into Barry's lap. "Better."

Jonas pushed his camera into Millicent's hands. "I want a picture with him, too."

Before long, Barry's lap was seeing more action than a department store Santa on Christmas Eve, as everyone vied for a photo of their own, each pose more outrageous than the last. After Jonas ran out of film, someone scrounged up the 45 of *Why Me?* and, after forcibly parting his lips, Barry was made to "sing along" with himself. One guy moved the corpse's chin up and down in time with the lyrics, and everyone howled with laughter.

Mal was sweating bullets now. This was bad. Very, very bad. "Okay, everybody," he shouted above the din of giggles and teenybopper pop, "that was fun, but we've really got to go now." He turned a pleading eye to Millicent, but she was busy cutting a lock of Barry's hair with a small pair of shears.

"Ooh! Good idea!" squealed one of the girls. "I want one, too."

Millicent handed her the scissors, and the fan took her souvenir.

The scissors were handed off from one kid to another until Barry was practically bald.

Mal felt tears tingling at the back of his eyes. He was so fucked. But he was only a freshman, so there was nothing he could do. He watched in mute, frozen horror as the last person to get the shears snipped off one of Barry's fingers, then waved it in the air.

"Look what I got!" the boy chortled.

This set off a frenzy, and within moments, Barry's body was obliterated from Mal's view. The partygoers resembled a pack of rabid hyenas, ripping, tearing, biting, and shredding the carcass until it was nothing left but bones.

"STOP!!!" Mal screamed, turning off the stereo and banging his hands on the speakers.

It took a moment, but they did. The bloodied, disheveled high-schoolers slowed, then stopped. They turned their heads, then their bodies, toward Mal. They stared at him blankly. Mal's heart skipped several beats—they looked like they wanted to rip him to scraps, too. A long, terrifying moment passed, then they began to blink and return to awareness.

"Oh, shit," Jenny cried. "Look at the sofa! My mom and dad are gonna ground me for life if we don't get this cleaned up."

Her friends murmured their agreement, then began to help her.

Barry, reduced to bones, was piled onto the far corner of the couch, with his grinning, fleshless head stacked at the very top.

Millicent and Jonas walked over to Mal, who was still petrified next to the stereo and staring in disbelief at the carnage. Mal was feeling dizzy. This was worse than bad.

"What now?" he asked Millicent. Even though this was all her fault, she was still the eldest and he looked to her for guidance.

Millicent shrugged. "Get the body bag," she replied.

Mal and Jonas went to the kitchen where, thankfully, the bag still lay open on the floor.

"At least he won't be so heavy on the way back," Jonas pointed out hopefully.

The boys hoisted the bag up and took it to the living room. Millicent helped them gather the bones into it, and Mal zipped it closed.

The partygoers were in serious cleanup mode when the trio exited, again using the back door.

...

It had been three days since Mal, Millicent, and Jonas decided to bury the body bag in the woods somewhere along the shortcut. It wasn't buried so much as stashed under a bunch of branches and leaves.

The police had been called to the Hackman Mortuary by Morty the following morning, the instant he'd discovered that Barry Birdsong's cadaver was missing. He never suspected his own children of being the body-snatchers, thank goodness, but Mal was being punished nonetheless.

He didn't come right out and tell his sister and friend that the pop star was haunting him, but he hinted at it. When neither one of them had any reaction, and they didn't say, "Me, too!" Mal kept his fears to himself. He found it so odd that Millicent and Jonas seemed to have no remorse, and little memory, about what happened. It was almost as if they'd been possessed by some strange pack-attack fever at the party. Mal convinced Jonas to hand over all the Polaroids, and the boys burned them in Jonas's backyard firepit.

The story was on the local news—about Barry's body going missing—but that wasn't the worst of it. The Hackman's reputation as morticians would surely be damaged, and Mal felt absolutely horrible about that. He knew how hard his parents had worked to build the business. The Beggar's Hole police force, all three of them, had been to the funeral home to take statements. They poked around, but they never ventured far enough off the property to be a threat. At least, not yet. Mal imagined other troops would come in, and maybe even bloodhounds.

That was all awful, but it wasn't the worst of it. Mal couldn't listen to any song on the radio, a record, or even a commercial jingle on TV, without it turning into the overly-sentimental strains of *Why Me?*. For the first day and a half, the haunting had been confined to sound. But now Mal was starting to see Barry Birdsong in every face. And this morning, when he was brushing his teeth, his own mirrored countenance had briefly turned into that of the handsome singer. He'd nearly choked on his Colgate.

Mal couldn't avoid radios and mirrors forever. What to do? He thought about getting a book on black magic at the library, or maybe even one with voodoo spells, but what good would that do? He was no warlock; he was just a ninth-grader with a year's supply of Clearasil and barely passable grades.

Salvation came in the form of Sid Greenblatt, Barry Birdsong's manager.

Greenblatt had been informed of the situation right away, so he didn't come to claim the body, but he did leave his phone number with Mortimer "just in case." Mal had seen the Los Angeles number written on the notepad his mom kept on the business office desk.

Mal waited until everyone was asleep, then he waited a couple of hours more before he crept downstairs to call Barry's manager.

The phone rang several times, each chime eerily mimicking the insipid, cloying melody of *Why Me?*. Just when Mal couldn't stand it another moment, his call was answered.

There was a clatter, then a gruff, sleepy voice. "Sid Greenblatt Enterprises."

"Um... Mr. Greenblatt please?"

"Speaking."

"Uh... you don't know me, but my name is Mal Hackman. I'm calling from the funeral home where," he said, his words coming fast and tumbling, "Barry Birdsong was taken when," he gulped, "he, uh, died."

"Okaaayy..." Sid said suspiciously.

"First, you have to promise me you won't tell my dad about this."

"Why? Who's your dad?"

"He's the mortician."

"What do you want, son?" There was a note of exasperation in the manager's voice. "It's late. If this is a prank call, I swear to God..." A beat. "I'm grieving, you know. Barry was one of my best."

"I'm sorry, sir," Mal said. "I'm not kidding around." He wasn't sure how to proceed.

"Look, I'm hanging up now."

"No!" Mal protested. "Please. I think Barry Birdsong is haunting me."

Unexpected laughter boomed through the phone lines. "That's my Barry, alright. What's he doing?"

Mal explained the situation, sparing no detail, then told Greenblatt about hearing Barry's song and seeing his face everywhere. "I can understand why he's mad at me, but what should I do?"

Greenblatt was quiet for a long time, but Mal could hear him breathing on the other end of the line. He hung on, feeling both nervous and hopeful. This could go either way. But even if Greenblatt decided to tell the authorities, Juvie was almost preferable to the torture of uncertainty, ghostly visitations, and the lyrics, "Why me? / How can this be? / Hear my plea / Don't cut down that tree." (Even at 14, the irony of those words was not lost on Mal.)

Finally, the manager spoke. "Let me get back to you."

Click.

Mal sat in his mom's faux leather office chair, staring at the large avocado green phone. What to do now? He tried calling Greenblatt right back, but the line was busy. Just as Mal was getting up to go back to his room, the phone rang. He snatched the receiver up as fast as he could, fumbling but catching it halfway through its loud trill. "Hello?" he breathed.

"It's me."

Mal's blood ran cold. It was Barry.

"Kid, are you there?"

Mal let out a long, shaky breath. It was only Greenblatt. "Yeah, yeah... I'm here."

"Good. I had to call Barry's astrologer. She knows what to do."

"What? What do we do?"

"I'm going to let you in on a little secret about Barry. He was... I don't know how to put it... kind of nutso. Barry absolutely *had* to complete a task once he started it. Everything from writing a song to finishing a steak dinner. He never, ever, left a tune half-composed, and he never, ever took home a doggie bag. You dig?"

"Um, I think so," Mal said. "Actually, no, I don't."

"It's some kind of obsession, or a compulsion, maybe. Barry had to see things through from start to finish, or it was a real bad scene. Gunta, his astrologer, told me she thinks the fact that Barry was a Virgo, coupled with the fact that he died with three shows to go on his tour, is the reason he's sticking around."

"Okay, but why is he haunting *me*? It's not my fault he didn't finish the tour. He's the one who wrapped himself around that oak."

"True," Sid agreed. "But you also kept him from completing the ritual of death—he can't rest until there's a funeral and he's buried in a proper cemetery."

Mal sighed. "Which is it? Does he need to finish the tour, or does he need to be buried?"

"Both."

"Okay, well, I'll show you where we stashed him, and you can take care of it."

Greenblatt seemed to be contemplating this, as there was another long, seemingly interminable pause in the conversation. "I'll tell you what. Barry's next gig was about 50 miles from you. He was set to play at Jinky's Tavern in Arkansas City. If you can deliver him..." After a barrage of protests from Mal about a math test and the lack of a driver's license, Sid muttered something under his breath, then said, "Okay, how about this? Express mail him to the tavern, and I'll take care of the rest."

"You won't tell my parents?"

"No, son. I won't tell." The manager chuckled. "I was something of a juvenile delinquent myself when I was your age. Have you got something to write with? Send the package to the tavern, to my attention. Here's the address..."

After hanging up with Greenblatt, Mal raided the petty cash envelope in the desk drawer for the postage, then looked around for a suitable bone-mailing box. He found one, broke it down, then tucked the flat cardboard under his arm, and made his way back up the stairs and into his bedroom. It was in the wee hours, but morning seemed ages away. He could hardly wait for the post office to open. Mal knelt at the edge of his bed, and prayed to God, then apologized to Barry for the whole situation. A moment after he crawled under the covers and closed his eyes, Mal was asleep.

...

He decided not to tell Millicent or Jonas about his macabre errand. He went by himself to the spot where Barry Birdsong's bones lay and uncovered the rumpled black body bag. It was crawling with dirt-bugs and mealy-worms, but the zipper was still fastened. Unfortunately, the bag was too big for the box, so Mal had to reach inside and take each piece of the skeleton out, one by one.

Rotting flesh and bits of cartilage clung to the ribs and the front of the skull, emanating a formaldehyde-tinged death stench that turned the boy's stomach inside out. But he had to do this, so he held his breath and made sure there was minimum fingers-to-skeleton contact as he arranged what was left of Barry inside the container. He expected the teeth to snap and the fingerbones to grab, but nothing happened.

He sealed the box shut, made sure the address was still legible, then headed to the small post office on the edge of town. It was a longish walk, and the clattery sound of skeletal remains shifting around inside made him worry that the package might arouse suspicion somewhere along its route. What then? He hadn't put a return address on, but with a popstar corpse missing and the postmark originating in Beggar's Hole, Mal knew his secret wouldn't last long if the box was opened before reaching its destination.

But he couldn't see any other choice, so he pressed on.

The post office had just opened when he arrived at 8 AM. Judy, a too-thin elderly woman who wore her long hair in a bun and kept her glasses perched on the end of her nose, greeted him warmly.

"Mal Hackman! Good morning, young man. Where's your mother?"

"She's not feeling so good today, so she asked me to mail this for her." Mal hoisted the heavy box onto the counter. "It's overnight."

Judy looked at the writing on the box for a long time, then squinted at him. "You forgot the return address." She plucked a pen from the front pocket of her smock. "Here, I'll add it for you."

"That's okay," Mal protested.

"Nonsense," said the postal lady brightly, writing out the address to Hackman Funeral Home in spidery script. "It's no trouble at all. Besides, you'll want this package to come back to you if there's any issue."

Not really, Mal thought. But he couldn't say anything, so he just smiled and nodded.

Judy hefted the box onto the scale. "Twenty-nine pounds, even. Heavy." When she slid it off the scale, the contents rattled. She frowned. "Sounds like something's broken already." She reached for a box-cutter. "Shall we take a look-see?"

Time slowed. The Muzak tinkling from the post office's puny speaker system morphed from an instrumental of William Shatner's *The Transformed Man* into Barry Birdsong's *Why Me?*. June's wrinkled face smoothed and took on masculine features. The bun on her head drooped, then formed into a textured, layered style. Barry.

Mal could feel bullets of sweat dotting his forehead. "Ummm," he said, eyes pleading, "It's okay. It's a puzzle. And I think I might have whatever my mom's got. I should get going." He mopped his brow with his sleeve.

Judy shrugged, then pushed the box aside. "That'll be $16 even."

Mal paid, strolled casually out, then broke into a dead run. He couldn't get away from his tormentor fast enough.

...

The haunting, both aural and visual, continued for the next two days. Mal was about to lose his mind. Then Millicent, as the Hackman family sat at the breakfast table, offered him a tendril of hope.

"Look at this," she said, holding up a section of the newspaper. "There's a Barry

Birdsong tribute tour kicking off tonight in Arkansas City."

Morty shook his head and sighed. "I hope his body is found soon. The sooner, the better." He looked over at his wife. "The locksmith is still scheduled for this afternoon, right Mabel?"

Mom nodded, then looked at Millicent. "The poor soul."

"Yeah," Millicent agreed, then started reading aloud from the article. "Birdsong's manager, Sidney Greenblatt of Los Angeles, California, has arranged for the last three dates of the pop star's tour to be performed by an impersonator, thereby fulfilling financial and legal obligations. Previously sold tickets will be duly honored." She grinned. "Groovy! I have a ticket to the show at Jinky's. Me and Jenny can still go!"

"As long as you keep your curfew, young lady," Morty said, turning his attention back to his scrambled eggs.

Mal was looking at his sister for any sign of fear, alarm, or even concern, but there was none. It was as if all memory of the desecration that had taken place at Jenny's party was erased for everyone but him. Yesterday, when Mal had seen Jonas in school and confided that he'd mailed Barry's bones off, Jonas merely shrugged, said, "Far out," then changed the subject.

Mal was starting to worry that there was something wrong with him. Like, maybe he was going crazy. Maybe this was some kind of nightmare and he'd wake up. Maybe...

He couldn't bear to think about it anymore.

Mal somehow made it through the rest of that day and the evening, but as Millicent's curfew approached, he thought he'd jump right out of his skin. He lay in his bed, trying to read *A Wrinkle in Time*, but the words on the pages kept reforming themselves into the lyrics to *Why Me?* Things were getting worse and worse, if that was at all possible.

Just when he was about to shut off the nightstand lamp and put his pillow over his head, Mal heard the front door open, close, then deadbolt. He listened as Millicent came up the stairs, passed his room, then went into hers, closing the door.

He got out of bed quietly, tiptoed across the carpet, then made his way to his sister's room. He rapped his knuckles lightly on her door.

She opened it a crack, peering out. "What do you want, blockhead?"

"Let me in," Mal whispered. "Please?"

She rolled her eyes and sighed, then ushered him inside. "What?" she demanded.

Mal smiled, trying to look nonchalant. "How was the concert?"

She sat on the edge of her bed and took her shoes off. "It was weird. The stand-in was pretty good, I guess, but he sang mostly in the dark. The spotlight stayed trained on this wooden chair with a cardboard box on it." She crossed her arms and ran her hands up-and-down her arms, as if she'd suddenly caught a chill. "Freaky vibe."

Mal breathed a sigh of relief. It seemed that Mr. Greenblatt was going to go through with the ritual, or whatever it was. Only two more concerts to go, and Mal would be free.

The next morning, he was the first to get the paper from the front porch. He yanked the rubber band off the bundle the moment he got inside, and opened the large daily as he walked toward the kitchen. No one else was up yet but it was only a matter of minutes. He spread the gazette out on the breakfast table and turned the pages quickly, scanning the headlines. Finally, he came to the Entertainment section—which, in their small town, was half of one sheet—and saw an ad for the two final Barry Birdsong farewell shows. One tonight, then another on Wednesday.

Mal let out a deflating breath. Wednesday. How could he make it till then? He considered playing hooky, saying he was sick, but being at home under the watchful eyes of his parents was probably not the best course of action. Mom could always tell when he was faking. But, in a way, he *was* sick—he certainly felt worse than he ever had in his short life.

...

The beleaguered boy went to bed on Wednesday night with full faith that he'd wake up the next morning and everything would be back to normal. But he couldn't sleep. He kept testing Greenblatt's theory in turns by listening to his transistor radio, reading from his book, and looking in the mirror. It was a barrage of Barry until, at exactly 11 PM, the pop star vanished.

"Whew!" Mal cried, wiping his happy tears. It was finally over.

He crawled under the covers, closed his eyes, and eventually, he dreamed.

Mal was at a concert. He was wasn't sure where, when, why, or who—only that he was in an audience of enthusiastic fans, applauding some singing superstar onstage. He was so far away from the stage he could see only a mobile dot and the music was a distant, indistinct wail. The crowd pressed in at Mal, pushing, pushing, crushing. Mal managed to get a knee up, then found footing on someone's body. He pushed himself up and up, until he was rolling on a wave of people, surfing ever-closer to the platform. The song came into focus, and the small, blurry face sharpened, then enlarged.

Barry Birdsong was onstage, wearing Western style clothing, tie-dyed, and all fringed. He strummed his banjo, and warbled the final refrain of *Why Me?* As the audience wildly cheered, the pop star's clothes faded, then his flesh fell bloodlessly away, disappearing into an otherworldly ether.

A skeleton stood there grinning, and nodding its skull. "Thank you! That's all, folks!"

The place went dark, then silent.

An urgent alert sounded. BEEP!

Mal opened his eyes. *Where am I?*

Beep, beep, beep!

It was his alarm. He was home, in his bed, and it was time to get up for school. Mal reached out, groping, and silenced the clock.

Thursday morning. Everything would be fine now.

Mal sat up, rubbing his eyes. He opened them, peering into the dawn-tinged dim of his bedroom.

He was not alone.

Mal gasped and sat up, trembling.

Perched on the edge of his bed was a skeleton. *The* skeleton. It regarded him with empty yet knowing sockets. Its teeth formed a grin, then the jaw moved up and down.

"Good start, kid," Barry said, snapping his twig-like fingers. "But now you need to find my flesh."

"Do You Believe in Tragic?"
A Teenage Death Song
Jeff Strand

Had two teenagers ever been more in love than Tommy and Susie? If you asked either of them, the answer would be an unequivocal "No." Sure, Susan was a rich girl and Tommy was a bad boy from the wrong side of the tracks, but when they stared into each other's eyes, they saw paradise. They laughed at other people who *thought* they knew what it was like to be in love. Those self-delusional losers didn't know squat about true love. Tommy and Susie were going to be together forever.

Chorus: *Forever, forever, forever, together foreeeeeeever!*

Because she loved him so very much, Susie begged Tommy not to participate in the drag race. "It's too dangerous!" she wailed. "You could get maimed! You could get killed!"

Tommy flicked his cigarette onto the ground. "What am I supposed to do, babe? Let the guys think I'd turn down a dare? Let them think I drive a car that's too unreliable to race? Let them think I'm scared of a messy death?" He shook his head in that manly way that he knew turned her on. "I have to do this."

"But... I'm going to have your baby!"

Tommy lit another cigarette. "What are you talking about?"

"I'm pregnant."

"You can't be. I held my breath."

"Then how do you explain me dreaming about building a crib last night?"

"Oh, my god." Tommy momentarily looked like he wanted to vomit, but then his face lit up. "We're gonna have a baby, darling! You and me! And I don't want you building a crib, even in your dreams. I'll build the crib with my own two hands, and I promise he won't fall out of it in the middle of the night. Babies have soft heads and it's not good for them to drop onto the floor."

"So you're not going to drag race?" Susie asked.

"We can't raise Little Tommy in a world where bullies think his daddy's a coward. I'm going to win that race, and you can tell our son how his father never backed down from a dare, no matter how foolish!"

Billy, the meanest bully in the valley, honked his horn. "Hey, are we here to race or what?"

Tommy gave Susie a kiss. It was the kind of love-filled kiss that most people couldn't even comprehend. That quantity of love simply didn't exist for most civilians, and quite honestly they'd be driven mad if it did, unable to cope with its sheer intensity.

He got in the car and started the engine, which took several tries because his automobile was so very, very crappy. Then he and Billy revved their engines at each other, until the referee shouted "Go!"

Tommy sped down the road. He was winning!

But his brakes...

Chorus: *Brakes, brakes, brakes, you've gotta check your brakes.*

You can't ignore brake maintenance.

Or there will be a consequence.

And you will need an ambulance.

Tommy crossed the finish line and let out a cheer. Then he pressed his right foot against the brake pedal, intending for the momentum of his automobile to lessen. But it didn't. He tried with his left foot and experienced the same lack of a result.

Everybody had thought it would be funny to conduct the drag race near a treacherous cliff, but nobody had anticipated a scenario where somebody's brakes failed. As Tommy hurtled toward the edge of the cliff, he knew that the only way he was going to live another minute was to turn the steering wheel.

But he couldn't turn the steering wheel to the left—there was a Dachshund in the way! And he couldn't turn the steering wheel to the right—there was another Dachshund in the way!

Tommy quickly rolled down his window and stuck out his head. "Susie!" he cried out. "I love you! Take care of Little Tommy for me!"

Susie's first thought was that she kind of wished Tommy hadn't blabbed about her pregnancy, since she had yet to quite figure out how she was going to tell her parents and deal with the scandal of being the town slut. Her second thought was pure horror as she watched Tommy's automobile—with Tommy inside—go over the edge of the cliff.

Chorus: *And Tommy plummeted.*
For almost nine hundred feet.
And when he struck the bottom.
His body was splattered meat.

Susie would have been horrified if she saw the actual moment of impact, because Tommy's eyeballs popped out of his head, and his left arm came completely off, and his ribcage basically just shot eight or nine ribs through his chest, and his neck burst open, and he bit his tongue. There was literally nothing about what happened to the father of her unborn child that would have made Susie happy. It was absolutely disgusting.

The teenagers all rushed to the edge of the cliff and stared down at the grisly carnage. The top of the car had been torn off, so they could see the geyser of blood spraying out of the vehicle.

Susie let out a wail of pure sorrow and heartbreak, a wail she knew would make the other girls jealous, because they knew deep inside that if their boyfriends died horrific deaths they wouldn't be as sad.

"It's okay," said Bobby. "It wasn't your fault."

"Why would it be my fault?" Susie asked.

"If he hadn't been distracted by calling out that he loved you, he would've been able to swerve to the left and still miss that one dog. But, again, it's not your fault. It's not like you forced him to race. Almost nobody blames you."

Susie wiped a single tear from her eye. "I will never love again."

And that was true for the next seven weeks. Then she met Peter. He was a bad boy from the wrong side of the tracks, and he didn't care that she was a godless tramp who'd gotten her boyfriend killed. When she gazed into his eyes, she forgot all about Tommy.

They kissed with great frequency, and it was refreshing that she didn't have to worry about getting pregnant since she was already knocked up. Though they'd only known each other for 38 hours, their love reached such amazing heights that songwriters couldn't come up with adequate lyrics to describe it.

Chorus: *Love, love, love, love, love.*
They were so in love.
Love, love, love, love, love.
And if you say it five times in a row.
That's objectively a lot of love.

"Bobby challenged me to a drag race," Peter told Susie, as he lit his cigarette.

"No! Don't do it! I can't lose you the way I lost... uh, that other guy."

"It'll be alright, babe. I have routine maintenance on my automobile. What kind of father figure would I be to Little Peter if I declined a drag race challenge out of fear that I'd suffer the same fate as his biological dad?"

"At least don't race near the cliff!" Susie begged.

"Then where would we race? The local racetrack? A deserted stretch of road? I promise you it'll be fine." He flicked the cigarette onto the ground and gave her a gentle kiss on the lips.

It was the last time he'd kiss her, or anybody, because later that night his lips would be smeared across the hood of his car at the bottom of the cliff. He'd been winning the race, and his car had been functioning properly, but he'd been distracted by the sight of a little boy in a wheelchair. *That poor little boy,* Peter thought. *I bet he never gets to drag race. I could bring some much-needed joy to his life if I gave him a ride on top of my car.* He smiled at the mental image of the crippled boy strapped to the top of his car, a great big smile on his face, arm raised in victory as he shouted "Faster! Faster!" Then Peter stopped smiling as he realized that his car was plummeting over the edge of the cliff.

In addition to the aforementioned issue with his severed lips, Peter's entire spinal column exited his body, and he lost three of his four major appendages. Had he survived, he would've been incredibly jealous of the boy in the wheelchair, who still had both legs even if they didn't work, but there was no time for jealousy before Peter's brain splattered all over the dashboard.

Susie's wail was even louder this time. "I will never love again," she said.

And this was true until she walked away from the carnage and saw Danny. He was a bad boy from the wrong side of the tracks, but his pompadour was exquisite, and it didn't bother him that Susie's boyfriend had just died a splattery death. Without a single word exchanged between them, they knew that theirs was a love that would last throughout the ages, a love that would inspire at least 47 songs, a love that would make Romeo and Juliet look like Salty John and the Slug Lady.

Susie knew that she shouldn't start making out with him before the police even arrived to investigate Peter's death, but there was no reason they couldn't hold hands. She took his hand in hers, and he took her hand in his, and no two people in the world had ever held hands so romantically. Neither of their hands were even the least bit clammy.

She knew that he'd be a great father to Little Danny. Their child wouldn't have his pompadour, at least not for a while, but she knew that Danny would teach their son to play baseball and drink milkshakes and build cabinets.

Not to drag race, though.

Never to drag race.

"Hey!" Bobby shouted at Danny. "I challenge you to a drag race!"

"Please, no!" said Susie. "Peter's body hasn't even stopped leaking yet!"

"I have a better idea," Danny told Bobby. "I challenge you to a switchblade duel."

"Please, no!" said Susie. "Knives can be dangerously sharp!"

The color drained from Bobby's face, but he couldn't turn down a duel in front of his fellow bullies, lest they chuckle. "Fine!" he said, taking his switchblade out of his pocket. He pressed the little button, and the blade popped out. But it wasn't a blade, it was a comb.

Three minutes later, Danny lay dead on the ground, bleeding from a dozen comb wounds. Susie sobbed and sobbed and sobbed.

Chorus: *Don't sob, Susie.*
Don't cry over Dan.
Don't sob, Susie.
You'll find another man.

But she didn't. Word got around town that Susie's boyfriends had a very short lifespan, and though she was hot, you have to be really, *really* hot to be worth dying for, and all of the guys in town agreed that she wasn't quite at that level.

When Susie's child was born at the nunnery, she was relieved that it was a girl, because girls didn't drag race. But Little Susie didn't conform to traditional gender stereotypes, and she displayed an early propensity for drag racing and switchblade duels. Susie wondered which one she'd die from first.

It turned out to be drag racing, at the age of sweet 16.

Chorus: *Why'd you drag race, Little Susie?*
You've broken your mama's heart.
Worse than you broke so many bones.
When you went over that cliff.
So, so, so, so, so, so many broken bones.

Yeah, yeah.

If this was a happy song, Susie would've gotten pregnant again and had a replacement child, but this is a teenage death song, even though Susie was now an old woman of 32.

She had many, many more tragedies in her life, and if this song bums you out with no real lesson beyond "Life can really suck for some people," then these depressing lyrics have done their job. Life is sorrow and grisly carnage. Goodnight, and remember that—unlike Susie's boyfriends and daughter—rock & roll will never die.

Stake Another Piece of my Heart
Staci Layne Wilson

He was there in the audience again.

"Mavis," he called to her, without saying a word.

The blinding lights, the fog of cigarette and pot smoke, and the shadows cast by the massive sea of humanity usually blended in a collision of visual haze when she was onstage, making it impossible to see details in the audience. But even way out there, several rows back, Mavis could clearly see his pale face, dark piercing eyes, and long, shining hair. This was the third night in a row he'd come to see her show, but this was the first time he'd spoken to her. How could he? She could hardly hear herself sing, let alone hear the sweet, beckoning whisper she imagined.

Imagined. That's all it was. As for him coming to see her three nights in a row, that was nothing unusual. She had quite a following. Mavis always attracted many groupies, male and female alike, but this man was older. It wasn't just the lines in his face and the silvery hair that hung in loose waves to his shoulders, it was something in his eyes. Something wise and knowing. Something *hungry*.

Mavis tossed her head in time to the driving beat of the music, trying to shake the image loose. She closed her eyes and made her guitar scream louder. She could feel the aggressively primal beat in every nerve ending. It came right up through the floor, shooting through her high-heeled leather boots, up her thighs, pulsing between her legs, tickling her belly, her breasts, and finally bursting out her mouth. She sang the next verse, roaring like a lioness and pushing her hips in time against her deep-red Fender Strat. Her henna hair flew in the wind created by the many fans placed around the stage, and it felt good.

It felt *so* good. This is what Mavis had dreamed of ever since she had been a young girl. Yes, she had lusted after Elvis and Jerry Lee Lewis, whose music she and her girlfriends loved. The difference was, her girlfriends wanted to be with those icons— Mavis wanted to *be* them.

And now she had her own top-charting band, Mavis & the Mixed Messages.

She tossed her silky, flat-ironed hair again and made the song come to an abrupt climax. She walked over to the mic stand and smiled, her light hazel eyes dancing over the crowd.

There were so many beautiful young men out there. She took deep breaths and her breasts heaved, barely contained in the leather halter top. It was festooned with beads and feathers, handmade by a fan in Laurel Canyon and given to her along with two fat joints of righteous weed.

"Who wants to fuck me?" she shouted, her challenge echoing out.

The crowd's cheers and whistles reached an almost deafening decibel level. Security guards had to beat back several of the people in the front row who attempted to rush the stage.

Mavis beamed at them. "You really do want me, don't you? Okay then, let's rock and roll!" She launched into another burning number, just she and her electric guitar up there before a crowd of over 18,000. And they *all* wanted her.

Little did they know she was a virgin.

...

Mavis spent most of the next day in her hotel room. Although she loved performing—lived for it, really—she did find the rock and roll lifestyle unbelievably dull at times. She began to get restless by late afternoon. She didn't have to do a sound-check that day, so she had time to kill. She'd tried to write a song, but it kept coming out like a Big Brother and the Holding Company rip-off. She took a bubble bath and slid her hands over her oiled body in the hot water, but she couldn't get into it. She ordered room service and nibbled at some mushy pasta. Finally, she decided to pick out her stage clothes for the evening's performance.

Mavis was lucky. She was blessed with a full-bosomed body that was easy to clothe. She looked as smashing in jeans and a t-shirt as she did in a crotchet mini-dress. She stood before the mirrored wall-length closet and let her terry-cloth robe drop. At 27, she was at the peak of her physicality. She wasn't stuck-up but she knew she had a killer bod. After pawing through a few outfits on the rack, she decided on a pair of go-go shorts and a top that was sewn from a genuine American flag. Probably illegal to wear, but she didn't care—her whole persona was about being provocative.

Sometimes she wondered, since she had so much time to think, if perhaps the perfection of her face and body was somehow a tangible symbol of her virginity. Maybe if she had sex, it would all fade. She smiled at herself in the mirror. *They all want me but I'm not gonna give it up.* She'd had countless offers to light her fire, but Mavis was anti-"free love." She was saving herself for someone special. Who? She didn't know yet.

She went over the set list. She liked to mix up the order of the songs every few shows or so, much to the annoyance of her band. Her biggest hit to date was *Vag Like a Vault*, but she was getting tired of that one. She had a few new tunes that were going down well— *Balls and Chain* and *Don't Bogart His Joint*—so those were circled as keepers.

...

"Colin, have you happened to notice an older man in the audience over the past few nights?" Mavis was sitting in the back of yet another stretch limo, riding to the stadium with her manager, Colin, and her bass-player, Sherman. The drummer and backup singers had already gone on ahead to the venue.

"No. Why, luv? Is he bothering you?" Colin was a big, burly Brit, always looking for a fight. He'd given up trying to get in her pants years ago, but was still jealously protective of her.

"No, nothing like that. I was just wondering. It's so strange to see anyone over the age of 20 at my shows. I guess he just kind of stood out."

"Hey, I'm over 20," Colin shot back.

"Me too—and so are you," Sherman said.

"Don't remind me," Mavis muttered.

"Oh, go on now," Colin guffawed at her false fret. "You'll be forever young."

"Don't trust anyone over 30," she replied, quoting the movie *Wild in the Streets*. "If you see that guy out there tonight, could you get someone to bring him backstage after the show? He's been sitting in the first loge seat, in the center, just to the right of the mixing board."

Colin gave her a humorless smile. "Don't tell me you're digging old hippies now?"

Mavis grinned and arched her thin, chestnut eyebrows up and down in an imitation of Groucho Marx, but inside she wasn't happy at all. She couldn't make sense of this feeling, which was beginning to border on obsession, for the strange fan. But she thought maybe if she could meet him, speak to him, she would see that he was nothing special and forget about him.

...

Mavis was fanning her face in the dressing room. The air conditioning couldn't begin to penetrate the inner heat she felt after a performance, but sometimes a strong breeze could. She'd put on a *really* hot show, and she could hear the audience screaming for more, stomping their feet and demanding an encore. They wanted her, and she couldn't wait to get back out there and give herself to them once again. Performing onstage was the best sex-substitute she could think of.

As she'd half-hoped, half-dreaded, he was there again. He sat in his loge seat, just watching her quietly with those onyx-like eyes of his. Unlike most concertgoers, this man did not mouth the lyrics to her songs or nod his head in time to the music. He didn't even stand up or shake his fist in the air. He just sat there, perched very tall and straight, hands folded in his lap, watching her. Although he was several rows back, the man's luminous face was like a beacon, drawing her eye several times throughout the night. Mavis was a professional though, and she never let on that she was distracted. The only indication that she'd seen him at all was to point him out to Colin after the last song, as she headed for her dressing room.

While she was onstage playing her encore, he would be brought back, and finally, she would know him. More and more, she was beginning to feel he was the one she'd been saving herself for. It was as if he'd found her using a map of the stars. Unerring fate.

Mavis took a deep breath and stood. She stepped out just as the guys' dressing room door across the hall was opening. She gave her band the thumbs-up and said, "Let's do it!"

She rushed through her two encore songs, and consequently made several mistakes when she noticed that he was no longer in the audience. He must be backstage, waiting for her.

She lingered until the guys went into their dressing room before going into hers. She opened the door to find...

No one.

Her dressing room was completely empty, which was unusual after a show. Colin could usually be found in there, one or more of her backup singers, wannabes from the record company, a couple of groupies who'd wheedled their way backstage, and so on. But tonight, it was quiet, and very still. It was almost as if the room was in a state of suspended animation.

Mavis walked inside and sat down in front of her makeup mirror. There, lying on the table was a single red rose. Held beneath the swell of the ruby bud was a tiny card, decorated with a border of curlicues. In the center was the handwritten message:

I am the one.

Mavis picked the card up and looked at it closely. She did not recognize the handwriting, which was so bold and deep, it was practically etched into the paper. Whose could it be? It had to be *him*. This lettering echoed his demeanor: bold and compelling. She wasn't sure how she knew, but she did. And the knowledge made her heart pound.

Just then, the door swung open. She sucked her breath in as she turned. She would do him right here in the dressing room.

It was Colin and one of the roadies.

"Sorry, luv. We tried to find that gentleman for you, but he must have left before the encore."

"That's okay, Colin," sighed Mavis.

...

As a storm tossed the chartered plane about in the night sky, Mavis couldn't help but think of Buddy Holly, Patsy Cline, and Otis Redding. For some reason, she mused, Thor, the Norse god of thunder, must not like musical performers. Or was it Zeus, the Greek ruler of the heavens? *I can't die a virgin.* She chided herself, wondering what kind of thoughts had passed through the minds of those other doomed performers.

But doom was not to be her immediate fate, after all. With a shimmy and a shudder, the plane landed safely on the runway of the Los Angeles International Airport.

She would only be in Cali for a few days, but she would be home. Mavis longed to see her beautiful Spanish style house again, to be inside its old, cool walls, to touch her bare feet to the tile and stone floors. She loved to hear the gusts of wind whistling through vents and to listen to the windows shake as the rain beat against them. The Canyon was a wild place, nestled in the hills and hidden away from the bustling Sunset Strip less than a mile away. Whenever there was a rare storm, it was almost as if the house was being seduced by the wind. *Can I come in?* The gale would whisper.

She'd always been able to hear words on the wind. One night when she was 13, the wind had said, *Be a good girl. Save yourself for me. I will come to you.*

That would have been the time to start seeing a kiddie shrink and lay off the homegrown. Instead, she found a guru and learned how to play the guitar. She ran away from home at 16, and a few years later, she had the number one hit in the nation: *Cross-Legged Mama.*

"Your car is here," Colin said, breaking Mavis's reverie. "Are you sure you want to drive? It's awfully wet out there. I can..."

"No thanks, Col," she said. "It's cool. If you could just get my bags delivered to me tomorrow, I would be eternally grateful." She hugged her manager and waved to the rest of her entourage. "See you freaks at the Forum. Hang loose," she called over her shoulder.

She headed for her candy apple red Mustang, which had been driven right up to the plane for her. The color matched her Strat perfectly. An old square dressed in an off-the-rack suit got out of her car and held the driver's door open for her. She slipped a few bucks into his hand and flashed him the peace sign. Such a gesture should have pissed him off, she thought, but he only smiled.

It was a lascivious smile at that. It seemed everyone and their brother wanted to fuck Mavis.

She slid onto the cool leather seat and eased the car into gear.

The steady rhythm of the windshield wipers was practically hypnotic, and before Mavis knew it, she was home.

She opened the wrought-iron gate with the remote control she kept in the glove box and drove in. As always, she kept an eye on the rear-view mirror, making certain that no one followed her. To say her fans were ardent was an understatement. As she drove up the winding, tree-lined driveway, Mavis noticed that some new flowers had been planted. Their colors were merely a blur in the driving midnight rain, but she was sure they would be beautiful.

They reminded her of the rose she'd been given the night before, and the giver of that gift. Would he follow her all the way to California? Would she search the Forum's audience for his face, and would she find it?

Suddenly, the rain stopped. It was as if a switch had been thrown, and the moon cast its cloudy cloak aside. Mavis cracked the window and breathed in deeply, the aroma of rain-kissed flowers filling her senses.

Coming around the final turn, her Spanish-style villa loomed into view, its white washed exterior and red tiled roof shimmering beneath the full moon. It was good to be home. Away from the constant barrage of sexual invitation.

Mavis pulled into the port, got out of the car, and went into the house through the side door that connected the dwelling to the garage. Mavis flicked the switch on the wall. There was a spark and then nothing.

The electricity had gone out.

She peered through the kitchen, across the dining room and into the den. The house appeared to be lit. Yes, there was the moon, but this light cast a warm, amber glow.

Candles.

There had to be hundreds of them. Mavis walked deeper into the house, following the trail of light. Her eyes were drawn to the staircase.

Him.

He stood there at the midway point, a resplendent, regal figure. His alabaster face was warmed by the soft candlelight, but the shadows cut eerie, dancing figures across his gaunt cheeks. His eyes were like burning coals, and his magnificent hair hung in silver waves to his proud, straight shoulders. He wore a white linen suit that fit like it was custom made. He wore no shoes on his feet, and in his arms was a huge bouquet of blood red roses. Slowly, he descended the stairs.

Mavis was rooted to the spot, speechless. She let him come to her.

I am the one, he'd written.

Yes.

Finally.

Now she knew without a doubt for whom she had been saving herself. In a *whoosh*, the past came crashing in... all those times the wind has whispered to her... it was him. *Always him.*

He stopped just in front of her and selected one rose from the bunch cradled in the crook of his right arm. He held it up and stroked her cheek with it, staring into her eyes. Mavis was spellbound. The rose slithered across her jawline, down her throat, and teased at her decolletage. Mavis unbuttoned her loose-fitting poet's shirt and opened it for him. The silky petals kissed her nipples and they swelled with excitement. Mavis caught her breath. She wanted to ask him who he was, how he had found her, what he was doing....

He put his finger to her lips, stopping all those unasked questions. She fell into his spell and followed him without hesitation when he turned and walked into the music room.

Flames were blazing in the fireplace, and the storm, raging anew, could be seen outside beyond the glass wall.

Fire and rain.

Several of her prized guitars were mounted on the far wall, and she looked at them, thinking about writing a whole new album all about the joys of sex... she knew that after tonight, she'd never play her old songs again.

The mystery man dropped the roses to the stone floor and took her hand in his. His flesh was cool and smooth, and his fingers were long and conical. He bent at the knees and brought her down with him onto the white fur rug that lay before the crackling blaze. He pushed the shirt from her shoulders and it fell in a feathery heap behind her.

Mavis eased herself onto her back and unzipped her tight jeans. She wanted to undress for him. She wanted him to watch her. She slipped the shoes from her feet. She was naked. The shadows cast from the dancing flames licked at her body and Mavis shivered with pleasure at the sensation of their warmth. She looked up with dreamy eyes and saw him, still on his knees and fully clothed, watching her. His eyes were like a cat's, reflecting back the light. Showing her nothing. He was so enigmatic.

She simply had to have him.

She caressed her angular hipbones, stroked her thighs, then let both hands travel back up and over the curve of her waist and the swell of her breasts. She felt him touch her quivering flesh. He had disrobed without her noticing. He held her so close, she couldn't see anything but she felt his fingertips caress the small of her back, roaming to her bottom. He lay her back and leaned over her, his silver hair framing his angular face. She raised up, her lips straining for his kiss. He kept just out of reach and looked at her with palpable hunger.

He kissed her neck. The sudden, sharp pain was exquisite. Mavis felt a warmth and realized he had penetrated her skin with his teeth. And then the waves came. She moaned with ecstasy, and saw supernovas shooting beneath her tightly closed lids. She felt as though she were being hurtled through space. She was hot and sweating in one instant, then ice-cold and shivering the next. She tried to open her eyes, but could not. She tried to move her arms, but could not. She tried to remember where she was, but could not.

And then the dream vanished.

She saw the blood. *Her blood*, shiny black in the candlelight, dripping down the chin of her undead lover.

"You're a vampire?" she asked incredulously.

He grinned, exposing long, ivory fangs.

Wow, I knew he was old, but this cat's gotta be at least a hundred. He looked good, though. She snuggled into him and ran her hands down his cold, firm body. *Finally, I am going to do the deed. I'm gonna get laid!* Her hand traveled southward, wanting to know what he felt like. She'd never actually touched one before.

She didn't know what to expect, but it wasn't this... this... *nothingness*.

He was smooth and featureless down there, just like a Ken doll.

She drew back and looked at him, questions in her eyes.

The wind whistled.

There were words.

My fangs are my phallus. It is the price of immortality, my love.

Mavis gasped. She looked down and saw that she, too, had the nothing smooth-nothing mound of skin below her waist. Even her bush was gone!

What the...?!

"You bastard!" she shouted, scrambling to her feet. "What have you done to me?"

All those years of abstinence, wasted! And now an eternity of virginity stretched before her. She was beyond furious. All her pent-up sexual frustration was unleashed in a single fluid motion as she reached for the nearest guitar. She yanked it from the wall-mount.

The vampire watched in open-mouthed amazement as Mavis brought the instrument down, body-first, onto the stone floor. The Telecaster splintered with a twang, falling away from the neck in great chunks.

His fangs retreated, shriveling in terror as Mavis came at him, brandishing the narrow shaft of wood... a jagged guitar-neck stake aimed straight at his heart.

California Screamin'
Renee Mallett

The curtains, such a bright red they were nearly lurid to begin with, were running slowly down the walls, melting. Winston eyed them with vague disinterest. He thought he felt the bed beneath him start to move and then realized that the entire room was spinning like a record.

This is a really bad trip, Winston thought with something almost like wonder.

The bed, rock-hard and encased in a coverlet nearly as red as the curtains, began to buck. So, it was the bed and the room, and they were both spinning in opposite directions. A frantic knocking sound began, increasing in volume until the hot, stale air of the hotel room seemed to reverberate with the noise.

I don't know what I'm doing in Kansas, Winston thought, not for the first time that night.

Suddenly the aging musician realized the room was filled with a sharp metallic odor, one that transported him to his youth, the years spent helping his dad in the family butcher shop. The curtains weren't melting. The walls were *bleeding*. Thick viscous liquid pooled in the bright spring green carpet, looking surprisingly festive, like Christmas decorations at a fancy department store.

Winston had one last thought before he blacked out, one of the most lucid and definitive moments of the entire three hours he had spent in room #2006 of the Hotel California.

This is all his fault, Winston thought before sliding into a welcome oblivion. None of this would have happened if it weren't for that guy, the one I thought was a fan.

...

The run-in with the fan, who was not a fan, had happened just two days earlier.

"Winston? Winston Wardley?"

Winston had been in the process of loosening his skinny black tie but stopped abruptly when he heard his name called. He knew that tone—knew it well, actually. It was, he had no doubt, the sound of a fan. Winston knew that after two hours under the stage lights the flesh-colored makeup he'd been caked with was probably more than a little smeary, but he was suddenly thankful he'd decided to walk back to the hotel in his white button-down and tie instead of changing at the venue. He smiled brightly at the man, surprised to see the guy was several years younger than himself.

"I knew it was you! Sally! Hey, Sal, come here!" the man called brightly, drawing looks from the few other people in the nearly deserted hotel entrance.

Like most of the others in the hotel lobby the man held the handle of a battered suitcase in one hand. It was just past midnight and his tone and the energy in his movements seemed a little too much for the hour. With the hand not gripping the pale blue plastic suitcase, he waved over a little girl, whose heavy-lidded eyes showed little interest in what her dad wanted to show her.

"I can't believe my family is staying at the same hotel as Winston Wardley," the man continued. "What are you doing here, man? This is, like, far out."

"Touring. Just got offstage a half hour ago." Even though the show had been a disaster, the venue more than half empty and the club owner complaining all night about losing money, Winston felt himself straighten up a little taller as he said it. Even after all these years it still felt good to be a working musician.

"Wow! I had no idea you were still playing music," Winston felt himself deflate as the "fan" kept talking. "Wish I had known; my dad used to love you guys."

The little girl had enough. She grabbed her father's hand and led him away from Winston, who was glad to see them go. As they approached the hotel elevator Winston heard the little girl say, "Daddy, who was that man?" The elevator doors didn't close fast enough to cut off the man's reply, painfully loud in the midnight quiet lobby, "That guy used to be famous."

"Mr. Wardley? You had phone calls while you were out."

Winston could tell the clerk had heard everything. From beneath his stupid little burgundy hat, the clerk looked blandly at Winston as he handed him two slips of paper and, without prompting, pulled a plastic phone from beneath the front desk. Winston scanned the names of the usual suspects: his agent and his wife. Finally loosening his tie, Winston counted silently backwards. It should still be early enough to call the coast. He pictured Norma-Jo in her bathrobe, fuzzy slippers on her feet, and even after all this time, cringed a little. Years ago, a lifetime ago now, the record label had told him getting married was good for his image but for the life of him he couldn't remember why they had thought Norma-Jo was the right girl for the job.

"Your check is late, and Bobby needs glasses," Norma-Jo said as soon as she answered the phone, knowing only Winston would call so late.

"I don't have any money. I'll send something as soon as I can."

"Don't give me that," she snapped just before hanging up the phone with a parting zinger: "You used to be famous."

Winston didn't bother to consider the time zone before returning his agent's call. Even after 10 years Winston still thought of Al as his "new agent." His first agent, his *real* agent, the one Winston and his friends had started with back in '49 was long gone. As with Norma-Jo, Winston couldn't pin-point exactly how Al had come into his life as his new agent. Winston's first agent had worn a suit and driven a Cadillac. Though for that matter, for a time, so had Winston. The new agent showed up in blue jeans. He was younger than Winston, something that vaguely rankled him, and he had a certain slickness to him that Winston had never quite trusted.

"Win, Win, Winston!" The new agent cackled. "Heard the show was bonkers."

"It was half-empty and a drunk asked where the rest of the band was," Winston told him.

Al sobered instantly, "Hey man, you were a draw in your day. You were. I gotta give you that. But the scene has changed. It's not 1952 anymore. It's barely even 1968 anymore. Time's relentless, man."

"I need money," Winston said flatly, cutting him off before he could dive further down that rabbit hole. "I need work."

"And I have got a gig for you," the new agent said smoothly, the joviality back as quickly as he had shut it off. "Different sort of thing. But good. A good, different thing. How do you feel about ghosts, Winny-Win?"

"What do you mean *ghosts*? Like a Halloween thing?"

"Nah, nah, man. It's an interview. The press! A feature, even. But at, like, a haunted hotel. It's what you need to get back on the map."

"What do I know about ghosts? What kind of press is this?"

"It's a music magazine," the new agent chortled. Winston started to think he was drunk or worse. "It'll be cool. You know, 'One night in a haunted hotel with Winston and the Tombstones,' only no tombstones. They know they can't use the band name; I made the rights issue very clear to them. Crystal clear. But still. You know. It's clever: haunted, ghosts, tombstones. But not the word tombstone. They know the label would come after that."

Winston wasn't sold. "What about a show? Even a small show."

"Listen, buddy, Winston," the agent continued. "You know I love your stuff, I grew up on your music, my dad was your number one fan. But your shtick? The duck's ass hair? The white shirt and black tie? The world has moved on, man. Little wifey at home with the kids while daddy-o is out with his guitar? That kind of goody-goody thing doesn't cut it anymore. I can't get anyplace to book you, even as a nostalgia thing. You need something a little edgy to show you've still got it. Ghosts and shit. Something the hippies can wrap their psychedelic minds around. One night at the Hotel California and you're relevant again."

"California," mused Winston, warming to the idea. "San Fran? L.A.?"

"Oakley! Uh, ...Oakley, Kansas. It's some Gold Rush thing. Where prospectors stopped on their way to the coast, dreaming big. California dreaming."

Winston cringed. Then he thought about Bobby's glasses.

"How much does it pay?" he asked hopefully.

"This is exposure, man," the agent said. "You can't put a price on exposure. If you mean, like, cash money? You're not thinking right. This isn't a paycheck. And I mean that really, as in you're not getting a paycheck. Discounted rate on the room. Maybe. I'll see what I can do. But think of the press. The right person sees this, and suddenly old Winston doesn't need the Tombstones. Let the label keep 'em, your name alone will be worth something. You've got a shot at a solo album. Not guaranteed. I just mean, you know, dream big. Like if the right person sees it, maybe it could happen."

"There's no such thing as ghosts," Winston said. "This'll backfire. Nothing will happen and they'll run a story saying even the dead won't show up for Winston, sans Tombstones. It'll be a big joke."

"Nah, man, no. I got a guy on the inside, he'll make sure there's something spooky to write about."

"You've got to have something else for me, is there anything else I can do?"

"Ditch the tie," the new agent told him. "Grow your hair long and get some bell bottoms."

"Tell the guy I'll do it."

...

It wasn't a guy, though. Stepping off the plane Winston was met by what looked like a kid, one who reminded him of a young Buddy Holly, if Buddy Holly had ever worn brown cords and an obnoxiously paisley printed shirt. Winston shoved his battered leather case into the kid's hands, thinking he was the driver. The kid wasn't expecting it, juggled the suitcase comically, and dropped it at his feet.

"Sorry, dude," he said, his voice a nasal high-pitched whine.

"We meeting the guy at the hotel?" asked Winston.

The kid looked confused for a moment and then said, "I am the guy. Photographer, too. I'm both guys."

Jesus, thought Winston, *now I know I'm old. Kid looks like a college freshman, not old enough to write for a magazine.*

"Thanks for doing this," the kid said, with his voice like locusts buzzing in the summer heat. "My advisor was really excited when I landed this for the school paper. His dad was a big fan."

I'll kill him, thought Winston helplessly. *I will fucking kill Al.*

The hotel was as much of a surprise as the kid. Winston had expected vintage wallpaper and reproduction antiques. Or maybe something Old West-ish. Rough boards and a swinging saloon door. But the lobby proved to be no different than any other hotel Winston had ever stayed at. And in a musical career spanning decades Winston had stayed at more than his fair share.

The place was almost screamingly average. Green carpet, beige-ish white walls. The clerk handed them the key without comment. Winston figured he thought they were father and son, but he was wildly glad he hadn't worn the shirt and tie he'd come to think of as his work uniform, just in case he was recognized. And through it all the kid just talked. Non-stop. About nothing.

"Wow!" the kid exclaimed, unlocking the door to their room. "Nice digs."

It was not nice digs. The blandness of the lobby continued into the room itself. Sturdy wooden furniture grew up out of the same lime green shag carpet found throughout the hotel. It could have been a room in just about any hotel. Pull off any interstate and you would have found a room just like it. Winston thought wildly about just leaving, walking out the door and telling his agent to stuff it. Then he realized he didn't have anywhere else to go. And he was getting a discount. Maybe.

The kid threw himself down on the bed furthest from the bathroom and tried to bounce a little. The mattress didn't give an inch. The kid didn't seem to mind but Winston's back hurt just thinking about it.

He noticed a price tag hanging out of the back of the kid's shirt as he unsuccessfully bounced. Winston figured that meant he'd bought that monstrosity of a shirt special for the occasion. He sighed.

"Hey, kid, what'd you say your name was again?"

"Lou."

Winston sang a few lyrics of "Louie, Louie," doo-wop style the way he had first heard Richard Berry sing it back when you could have found a song by Winston and the Tombstones at the top of the charts. "You don't look like a Lou," he broke off, interrupting himself.

Winston saw the kid debate something with himself before finally cracking a sheepish grin.

"It's, like, my *nom de plume*, my real name is Kermit. I want to make it as a journalist. Like Hunter Thompson, you know, like that book he did with the Hell's Angels? That's what I want, I want to get right into the middle of a story. I figured I needed a cool name. Kermit's not going anywhere, no place cool, but Lou might."

Winston couldn't help but return the smile. The kid was growing on him. A sharp rap at the door made them both pause.

"Room service," croaked a voice like something that had just dragged itself from a crypt.

Winston looked questioningly at Lou, the kid shrugging. Opening the door he found a squat little pumpkin of a man, wearing a dull orange plaid suit that looked to be covered in ashes or dirt. As he wheeled the cart into the room, he gave Winston a surreptitious wink. Winston realized this must be Al's inside guy.

"Your meal, sirs," he said, again in the same ridiculous put-on rusty voice.

"Are you for real, man?" Lou said, looking a little confused but starting to laugh just the same.

Winston had a sinking feeling. He lifted one corner of the covered plate and tried to figure out what was going on. In the background he heard Lou asking the page if he knew he had black shadow under his eyes. A thick green slime, dotted with bugs, oozed over the plate. Winston poked it experimentally. Plastic. Plastic bugs in Jell-O. Abruptly Winston dropped the cover back over the mess.

"Wrong room," he said. "We didn't order room service."

"But the call came from this room," the ghoul intoned as if from the depths of a deep black well. "You're not telling me something... *unseen* made the call, are you?"

"Wrong room," Winston said through gritted teeth, grabbing the jerk by the arm and swinging him out into the hallway. He was going to kill Al when this was over, should probably do it anyway just for sending him to Kansas.

"That was crazy," Lou said. "What do you think that was about?"

Winston didn't answer him, he tried flicking the television set on but didn't even get static. He checked that it was plugged in and then banged experimentally on top of the set. Nothing. He realized it was going to be an even longer night than he first thought. As if he could read his mind, Lou cracked that grin again and pulled a bag of grass from his pocket. After watching him unsuccessfully try to roll a joint, dropping chaff all over the technicolor red bedspread, Winston snatched it from him. Mostly seeds and stems. He gave the baggie an experimental sniff but the crap the kid had brought was so weak he could barely smell a thing from it. There was a saying about beggars and choosers though. One-handed, Winston rolled the joint and took the proffered lighter. First hit he wondered if someone had sold the kid a bag of oregano but after the next one, he started to feel more mellow. He took one more puff and passed it to the kid. They each lay on their own beds staring at the ceiling and smoking.

"What's the deal with this place?" Winston asked after a while, not really interested but wanting to pass the time. "Lady in white haunt this room since her suicide after being jilted at the altar? Or are we supposed to say Bloody Mary three times in the mirror?"

Lou started to laugh; as bad as the weed was, the kid was definitely feeling it. "You don't know anything about ghosts, do you?" He finally spluttered, handing what was left of the joint to Winston.

"Should I?"

"Your agent said you were an expert. That you knew all about this place. Said you loved that stuff, that's why you picked the name Tombstones for your band."

"Record label picked the name, kid." Winston told him. "The head guy over there back in the day loved those Abbott and Costello movies. You know, *Abbott and Costello Meet Frankenstein*, *Abbott and Costello and Boris Karloff* and whatever. That's why the label owns the name and not me. I don't even believe in ghosts."

"There's no ghosts at the Hotel California."

"No shit. There's no ghosts anywhere."

"No, I mean it." Lou said, suddenly earnest. "It's not a ghost. The prospectors stopped here, like a hundred years ago, just for the night, on their way to the gold rush. Only for some of them, the hotel was, like, the real treasure. People say, just for some people, this place gives you exactly what you always wanted."

"That's bullshit," Winston said flatly. "Nobody says that. If people said that the place would be packed every night and there'd be a line out the door waiting for a chance just to sit in the lobby."

"No," Lou was really warming up to the story now. "Only some people get stuff, very few. Most people, nearly all of 'em, they just get a night at the hotel. But some other people? They see the reaper. You see the reaper, you get nothing. You get a coffin."

The kid was getting really animated. He propped himself up on one arm on the bed and was staring intensely at Winston. Winston couldn't figure out where he was getting the energy. The air, perfectly normal if a little stale when they entered the room, now felt thick and cloying, like trying to breathe through a wet blanket. He thought he smelled something rotten, and his stomach suddenly seized.

Sick, thought Winston. *I'm going to be sick.*

He tried to turn on his side, choosing to puke across the cheap bedspread instead of on himself but couldn't even muster the strength to roll over.

"Don't fear the reaper," Winston mumbled. "It's only make-believe."

Whatever moment of clarity the kid had felt was now over. He was twisting around slowly on his tiny twin bed, eyes shut like there was something he didn't want to see.

"I can dream, can't I?" the kid asked, barking the words harshly. "I just want to be part of the story. What do you want, Win? What do you dream?"

I want to be somebody famous again, Winston thought helplessly.

The broken television sputtered to life. On screen Winston saw the crimson and clover hotel room he was currently laying in. But the room wasn't right. Everything looked like it was bathed in a moonlight cocktail, the image skewed in such a way that it hurt to look at. Every line in the room, every article of furniture, the corners where the walls came together, was just off in some way that made Winston want to grind his teeth until they shattered. He wanted to look around, try to figure out where the camera must be placed but couldn't turn his head. It felt like it was gripped in a vice, slowly growing tighter and tighter. His eyes started to bulge from the sockets, and he wondered wildly if they or his skull would burst first.

Just as suddenly, the pressure was gone. Winston staggered to his feet.

Gave me laced dope, Winston thought, forgetting that earlier he had been just as convinced the kid had been catnipped.

A staccato of cracks, like someone methodically cracking each knuckle, drew Winston's attention to the kid's bed. Lou's body jerked with each pop, as if tiny fireworks were going off down his spine, unseen. With one final snap his head twisted backwards, an impossible contortion, and he grinned at Winston's slack face.

"What do you dream, Winston?" the kid shrieked, scuttling off the bed and across the floor backwards like a spider.

Winston didn't know if he tripped or fainted but it happened in slow motion, like falling backwards in a swimming pool. The carpet squelched unpleasantly when Winston fell into it, soaking his blue jeans with some kind of stinking oily ooze.

Jell-O? thought Winston stupidly, *how'd Al do this?*

The spider thing lurched up the wall in a series of quick jerky movements, settling into the dark corner above the hotel room door. Its head spun around five or six more times. Every time Winston thought it was done it would start spinning again. With one final pause, its mouth opened in a wide rictus as if to sing but instead the distorted acid bleat of an electric guitar roared out.

Fuck this, thought Winston. *I used to be famous.*

He pulled himself up from the stinking carpet and grabbed the lamp from the night table. It was long and smooth, with a solidness to it that surprised him, reminding Winston of how the microphone stand had felt in his hands back in the day when he could fill a club with a crowd of teenage girls chanting his name. With a roar no fan of the Tombstones would ever believe could come from the vocal cords of Winston Wardley, he raised the lamp above his head and flung it at the monster.

The shrill bray of the thing cut off instantly. Winston grabbed the lamp and beat the thing until it stopped twitching. When his arms were too tired to keep going, he threw himself onto the bed. Winston thought the thing about what a bad trip this was. Then the thing about Kansas. Right after realizing the curtains were not melting, it was just bleeding walls, Winston started to feel very tired and shut his eyes.

...

A minute. An hour. An eternity. Sometime later Winston was roused by a fire alarm he at first mistook for a rallying cry from the Lou thing. It was icy in the room and the sprinklers rained down a flood of cold water. It should have been refreshing but Winston felt like something dragged up from a trench under the ocean. He slid off the water-logged coverlet, landing on his knees beside the bed, as if about to pray. Instead, he pulled himself up on shaky legs, like a sailor just returning to solid ground after a very long time at sea. Blankly he surveyed the room. It looked like some hippie rock star had gone wild. The last time Winston had woken up in a hotel room that looked this bad, the label had made him marry Norma-Jo. Lights were knocked over, flickering madly, television playing static, monster mash blocking the door. Winston looked closer at the bloody pulp and sagged. No monster, just a kid, probably around the same age as his oldest son.

The white noise on the television skipped. Walter Cronkite, backed by a map of the world, filled the screen.

"Sad news today from Kansas," the news anchor said soberly. "Winston Wardley, the 1950s crooner who had faded into obscurity, is dead by his own hand after killing aspiring journalism student Kermit Anderson. The murder-suicide appears to have been the outcome of a drug fueled party. No one seems to know what the former star was doing in

Kansas. Representatives of the one-time chart-topper have offered their condolences to both families and said the entire catalogue of Winston and the Tombstones recordings will be re-released. And that's the way it is."

The anchor said the date, which Winston was fairly sure wasn't until tomorrow, and signed off. For a brief moment Winston could picture the date chiseled onto a grave below his name. He wondered if there was any chance they'd bury him in Palm Springs, and which Winston and the Tombstones lyrics Norma-Jo would pick for the memorial. The set went back to static.

Winston straightened up tall and walked steadily to the room's one window. He pulled the red curtains, wet and tattered, back to let the sunshine in. Humming a little tune, he pried open the window and slipped halfway out to view the distance to the parking lot below. It would do.

Winston gave the window frame an affectionate pat, softly crooned, "I'm a believer," and then tipped himself head-first onto the asphalt below.

It's My Party, and I'll Die if I Want To
Darren Gordon Smith &
Staci Layne Wilson

SPRING 1964

Gabe clutches the steering wheel of the 10-year-old red Ford Thunderbird convertible, turning it this way and that. If only he could actually drive it instead of just sitting here in the driveway. But there are other things—better things—to be grateful for.

For instance, sitting in the passenger seat beside him is the girl of his dreams, Anna. Gabe can see her slim ankles just below the fold of her pedal-pushers, and her sweater is tighter than it should be for a girl her age. Not that he's complaining—besides, Gabe is the same age, so that makes it okay, he figures. Her strawberry blonde hair is shoulder-length, and the ends flip up just like *The Patty Duke Show*'s titular star.

Anna fiddles with the radio, but all they're getting is static. She blows a big bubble with her chewing gum, pops it, and then deftly reels the explosion back in with her tongue. "I can't believe you don't know *Twist and*

Shout. It's on the radio, you know, like everywhere, all the time."

Gabe smiles at her, even if she is a bit of a know-it-all. "Okay, you win, Anna. You're a bigger Beatles fan than me. But someday, I'm gonna interview them. Even Ringo."

"And even Pete Best?"

"Him, too." Then he reconsiders. "No, I shouldn't say all that; it sounds like a bunch of big talk."

Anna reaches out and puts her hand on his forearm. "No, it doesn't. Look, Gabe, you're already the best writer in our class. I wouldn't be surprised if I open up the paper someday and there you are interviewing Dylan. Anyway, what's wrong with you and me having big dreams? I mean, I wanna be a famous photographer."

Gabe sees the earnestness in her eyes. Her big, blue, beautiful eyes. They're like a magnet, drawing his face closer to hers. To his surprise, Anna doesn't move away. Just as their lips are about to meet, a screech of static bursts from the radio, ruining the moment.

Anna's hand moves for the dial. To Gabe's dismay, she doesn't turn it off. She turns it up.

"Don't you just love this song?"

"I don't think I know—"

"Shh!" Anna unfolds her legs and stands up in the corroded convertible, grooving to the music.

Gabe watches, transfixed by her swiveling hips.

"Anna!" Someone screeches nearby. "What in God's holy name are you doing?!"

Anna stops and turns. "Nothing, Mother—"

Gabe takes his hands off the steering wheel. He's never met Anna's mom, but he's been told that this rust-bucket is Wanda's pride and joy. He's seen her driving through town in it on her way to the local tavern more times than he can count.

Wanda, wearing nothing but a ratty housedress, pads over to the car, her pale bare feet practically glowing in the twilight. Her bouffant hairdo makes a shadow across the hood. "This is the thanks I get for raising you, taking you to church every week, and going through hell for you for 14 years?"

Anna sighs. "I'm sorry, Mom."

Wanda puts her hands on her hips. "Look at you, running down my car battery, out here strumpeting with some strange boy. And you better not have been out here wasting more film with that stupid camera of yours!"

"No, Mom, I didn't—"

"And do you know what time it is, young lady? Turn that Devil music noise off!"

Anna gives Gabe an embarrassed, apologetic smile.

"I guess," Gabe says, "I should go." He gets out of the car, careful not to slam the door behind him even though it weighs more than he does.

Anna gets out, too. "I guess I'll see you in Algebra tomorrow."

Gabe sings, "Yeah, yeah, yeah!" Beatles-style.

Wanda glowers, grabbing her daughter roughly by the arm, then pulls her toward their towering, strange house.

Gabe sighs, then decides to head home where he has the latest issue of *Rave* waiting to be read. As he shuffles through the gathering darkness, Gabe looks over his shoulder at Anna's home. The kids call it The Witch House, and Gabe has no idea how Anna can stand to live here. It's so creepy.

The dilapidated mansion, so out of place in the otherwise modest residential neighborhood, has a grand, domed colonnade fashioned in the shape of an ancient Roman temple and is two stories high not including a small octagonal room at its apex. Slate gray stone makes up the outer part of the first floor, then the girth of the structure is corseted with dark, ornate fish scale wood siding. The wood gives way to a beaten copper-sheet coating on the gable, and lastly, a spiky needle spire shone a narrow beacon straight up into the sky.

Gabe fully believes the place is haunted, cursed, and Satanic all at once.

SUMMER 1967

There was a time not too long ago, when Gabe had been terrified of this place. And now here he is, standing at the front door.

He wonders whatever happened to the girl who used to live here... Anna. Shortly after he'd met her, Gabe's dad, a military man, had been transferred to Germany and the whole family was forced to go. Gabe wrote to her a few times, but Anna never answered. Now that he's back in the States, he's been thinking about her again. He knows she doesn't live here anymore, but he hopes she hasn't gone too far.

Just a few months ago, a rock band manager named Sid Greenblatt bought the place and turned it into party central. Gabe would be sure to ask what happened to the previous tenants, but right now he has to focus on the task at hand. *Work before women*, he thinks.

From inside the house, loud music throbs. Gabe knocks on the door. No one answers.

After a few more knocks he tries the knob. It's locked.

Gabe cocks his head at the oblong mirror in the middle of the door. He and his friends used to think it was there to trap and reflect evil spirits. But now, it's only showing a baby-faced 17-year-old with a pimple on his chin. Even so, Gabe thinks he'll fit in with this hip crowd. He's been growing his hair and even cultivated sideburns. He wears a string of love beads, leather sandals, blue dungarees, and a tie-dye shirt half-concealed by his dad's old sport jacket. In his hand is his brand-new reporter's notebook, college-ruled.

He knocks again, then searches for someone to let him in. Turning to his left, he sees an outdoor hangout spot complete with a fire pit and beanbag chairs, but there's no one there. He takes a few steps back and peers up at the highest balcony.

There's an unsmiling long-haired hippie looking down at him, wearing faded hip-huggers and nothing else. Gabe instantly recognizes him. He's the reason Gabe is there.

Atom Anderson is the leader of The Near-Death Experience, an up-and-coming acid rock band that just released their first album. They are gearing up for a U.S. tour and Gabe is determined to interview them.

He's been writing music reviews for some small underground fanzines, but he thinks this interview could be worth something—it could even set him on his career path.

The loud music ends with a crescendo. Then there's laughter, and scattered applause. *Hmm, the rest of the band must be practicing,* Gabe thinks. *I'm in luck.* Taking advantage of the break, Gabe dashes to the doors and knocks again.

Within seconds, it's pulled open.

Standing there is a bare-breasted woman wearing cutoff shorts. She gives Gabe a lazy, hazy smile. "You're so young, so cute. Come on in." She steps aside.

Gabe is grateful, but suddenly feels shy and uncertain about how well he actually will fit in. Is this a nudist colony? He's never seen boobs up-close and in-person before.

"I'm Angel-Dust," announces the woman, pulling the tube-top up from her waist to cover herself.

"Um, Gabe."

They walk down a long hardwood hall and into a crowded den. The whole place is enveloped in incense haze, fumes from a hookah, and smoke from about a hundred smoldering joints. Gabe sees an old-fashioned upright piano in a far corner with a Victorian chair in place of a bench, and assorted music-makers—a tambourine, a pair of small bongos, and a pan flute—lay scattered around the room. The red couch is made of worn velvet and there's a proliferation of pillows on the floor. Gabe sees an assortment of partiers, most of them female. *Those must be the groupies I've read about*, he thinks, taking out his notebook and writing the observation down.

"Don't be shy, Little Man," Angel says, the late afternoon sun streaming in through the windows turning her long, straight hair a brilliant yellow. "Go join the party."

"My name is Gabe," he corrects her, feeling his face flushing red.

"Well, I'm going to call you Little Man," says the groupie, giving the boy a pat on the head.

"I'd really rather you didn't. You see, I'm a journalist, and I—"

Dashing down the rickety stairs, Atom bounds into the room. He steps right up to Gabe, sees his notebook and scowls. "Hey, kid, I already told you: no interviews."

"No sir. I mean, no *man*. It's cool. I'm not trying to get an interview out of you. I was just here to, um..."

Angel puts her arm around Gabe. "He's come to make the scene with us here, baby. Come on Atom, he's so cute. Can't we keep him?"

Atom smiles the impish rock-god grin that's going to make him famous. "Alright. But not if he gets too big to flush down the toilet. Anyway, it's Sid's place, not mine." He lasers back in on Gabe. "But remember—"

Gabe stuffs his notebook into the inner front pocket of the sports coat. "I got it, no interview. Unless you change your mind."

"Don't press your luck, kid."

Ziggy, the shaggy-haired drummer for the band, strolls into the room arm in arm with a gorgeous Bardot-class beauty who is so drugged-out she looks as though she has no idea where she is.

Ziggy spots Gabe. "Hey, man, you made it. Is Atom giving you a hard time?"

Atom frowns. "Wait. Ziggy, you invited this, this... reporter?"

"Chill, brother," Ziggy drawls. "The young dude is cool. He wrote this mindfuck liner note for..." He chins toward Gabe. "Who was that again?"

"Space Goats." Gabe looks worriedly at Ziggy's companion. "Hey, is she okay?"

"I'm Mary Juana," slurs the girl as she plops down to the floor, then sits up, staring into space.

Ziggy glances down at her with an indulgent smile and a shake of his head, then turns his attention back to Gabe. "Yeah, that's it, Space Goats, those far-out jazz cats.

And this motherfucker here, he's an Old Soul, Atom. He writes like he's been hip to celestial bodies and the aliens since time began."

"Actually, I was just being satirical. I don't really believe in..." Gabe feels Angel squeezing his upper arm. She's shaking her head. "Um, yeah," he says quickly, "I'm hip."

Atom chuckles, then wanders into the crowd, making a beeline for a square girl who looks like she got lost on her way to the Alpha Kappa Alpha sorority. Gabe watches as his quarry disappears into the fleshy crowd.

Ziggy snaps his fingers to get Gabe's attention back. "How can you be satirical?! When the fate of Mothership Earth is in the grubby little cricket hands of the beasts from Eos?"

"No, man, that's serious stuff," Gabe agrees, his words coming so fast they tumble over each other. "Hey, no judgment here."

Ziggy flashes Gabe a peace-sign. "Cool, brother."

Gabe hears a deep female voice yelling from the next room. "Ziggy, where are you? I worked out the bridge and the last chorus."

Ziggy takes a pair of banged-up drumsticks from his back pocket. "Right on, coming!" He pats Gabe on the shoulder. "Allie's on to something, gotta go."

So, the whole band is *here*, Gabe thinks. *Groovy.*

The scrawny percussionist makes tracks, leaving Mary sitting cross-legged on the floor staring at the wall.

Coming from yet another room in the mansion, a braless brunet wearing a holey orange crochet minidress and nothing else, sidles up to them. She glances down at Mary. "Whoo, she is flyin'!" The groupie gives Gabe the once-over. "I'm Micro-Dot," she says, "Got any weed?"

Gabe is about to mumble that he doesn't, but Angel interjects. "This is Little Man! He's a writer."

Dot cocks her head. "Oh?" She beams. "Nice to meet you, Little Man Writer. Can we get you anything? Coke, rum, poppers, Maui-wowie?"

"Maui what?"

Angel winks at him. "Forget it. Dot, let's go fix something that'll blow the kid's mind."

"No, thanks, I don't want to be any trouble," Gabe protests, but Angel and Micro-Dot are already walking away arm-in-arm, giggling.

With the friendly groupies gone and Atom in the corner hitting on the sorority girl, Gabe is left alone with Mary, who is still staring intently at nothing. "So, how do you know Atom?"

"How do *you* know Atom?" Someone echoes. It's a blue-eyed man wearing sandals, golf-pants, a polo shirt, and a purple beret. Without waiting for a reply, the guy introduces himself as Sid Greenblatt. "I own the place."

"I'm Gabe. I hope it's okay that I'm here."

Sid gestures at the assorted youths lounging in the den and the courtyard beyond. "Everyone is welcome here." Sid extends his hand for a give-me-five soul shake.

"Thanks." Gabe tries to return the hand-jive, but fails. He stuffs his hands into his pockets. "So, you manage Near-Death?"

Sid nods, then strokes Mary on the head as if she were a beloved pet.

"I write about rock and roll," Gabe says. "Atom said no interviews, but you know him better than I do. Do you think he'll let me get a few quotes for the record?"

Sid smiles. "Good luck with that."

"Maybe *you'd* give me some quotes?"

Sid shakes his head. "Sorry, the witches have sworn me to silence."

Witches. "So, it's true? This place is haunted?"

"I misspoke. Witch. There's only one. And speaking of which, you might have more luck talking to Allie."

Gabe sighs. "But I heard Allie's like 'all-about-the music, screw reporters'."

"You're right, on both counts. She lets the music do the talking, but she does have a soft spot between her legs for cubs like you." Sid checks his large, clunky wristwatch. "But hold that thought, my young Edward R. Murrow. I've got to run an errand. And don't worry, I'll add your name to the list when I score the peyote."

"No thanks, I'm just here to—" But Gabe's words fall on air as the hasty homeowner turns and makes his way to the front door.

Gabe looks down at Mary. "Sid went out to score. He'll be back soon. But I don't think you should take any more—"

"Huh?" Mary grins at Gabe with tears glistening in her eyes. She rises to her feet, shakily.

Suddenly Atom is there putting his arm around Mary to steady her. He looks at Gabe. "I said no interviews, but I don't want you to leave empty-handed. Why don't you take one of the groupies? I don't mind sharing; besides, I'm working on Muffy." Atom nods toward a trio of identical blondes, each wearing tweed knee skirts, pastel cardigans, and modest kitten-heels.

"Which one is Muffy?"

Atom winks. "Does it matter? I'll probably bag all three of those uptight chicks before this party's over."

Angel and Dot return, carrying huge, frothy drinks enveloped in swirling clouds of dry ice.

"You want a drink? We made a special brew, Atom," Angel says.

Atom takes it, then turns toward the college girls. "I fixed you a drink for your muff, I mean, for you, Muffy." He walks over to the collage of blondes.

Gabe watches as the girl in the middle, presumably Muffy, puts her nose to the glass, sniffing it like she's smelling dog dirt. "What's in this?"

"I don't know," Atom says. He turns and calls out, "Hey, Angel, what's in this?"

Angel ignores him.

Dot sighs and says to Gabe, "What does he see in those square chicks?"

Gabe shakes his head, but the inference that he's also a square is not lost on him. *Need to grow these sideburns longer,* he thinks.

Angel, in one large gulp, downs the rest of her drink. "To hell with Atom then. From now on, I'm sticking with Ziggy. And Allie." She turns to the front door, which is opening. A dark, handsome man walks in. "And whoever that is, too."

Gabe shifts uncomfortably from foot-to-foot. Mary leans on him, drooling slightly.

Gabe watches Atom for a moment, then he sees Ziggy coming back with Allie in tow.

Allie strikes Gabe as an intensely serious, enigmatic woman who gives off dark vibes— if Gregor Rasputin had no beard or penis, and played a single-coil Strat, she could be his twin.

The band members brush by Gabe and the groupies, making a beeline for Atom.

Allie says, "Hey Atom, you've got to come hear this."

Ziggy claps his hands. "Yeah, man, we worked out the bridge to *Pipe Dreams*. We've even got an ending, if you like it. Come listen."

Atom gives his fellow musicians an obligatory glance. "Far out, I'll join you cats later. Right now, I'm gonna bag this USC daddy's girl."

Muffy huffs, "Hey, I heard that! And so did Blair!"

The blonde to Muffy's left nods her head. "Come on, Muffy, let's get out of here!"

Ziggy sidles up to the girl. "Blair, great name. Hey, guess what? I have a Ferrari."

Blair's green eyes grow wide. "You do?"

Ziggy puts his arm around her. "Sure, come on outside and I'll show you."

Blair takes a step, but Muffy stops her. "Wait, maybe I should go with you. Then we've got to leave, right, Blair?" She turns to

142 | ROCK & ROLL NIGHTMARES
Along Comes Scary

her other lookalike friend. "Right, Cindy? We're headed to a party in Pasadena."

Atom's smug expression drops. "But... Muffy, my darlin', I've got a Mercedes 600 W100 outside. Just like Elvis's. You want to see it?"

Muffy's face lights up. "Really?"

Atom and Muffy, and Ziggy and Julia, walk out the side door.

Angel downs the rest of her misty concoction. "If he brings those prissy Goldwater girls back, I'm gonna mix him up something he never forgets."

Gabe takes a step back as a dour-faced woman with an afro, wearing a camo bikini and combat boots sweeps by him and into the hallway.

He sees a pretty, petite strawberry blonde girl coming the other way, then both women disappear into another room. Asking no one in particular, Gabe says, "Does anyone know that girl?"

"Diana? She's been here partying for a couple of days," Allie replies.

Gabe considers this. "No, the other one."

Allie shrugs. "I don't know her name, but she's some chick photographer. A friend of Sid's."

Angel elbows Gabe. "She's a young go-getter like you, Little Man. And she must've used up at least 10 rolls of film, getting shots of just about all of us."

Gabe is intrigued. "Allie, did she get your picture?"

"At least a dozen." Allie rolls her eyes.

"Hey," Gabe ventures. "Would you consider giving me a quick interview? I mean, I'm just a freelancer, but I've gotten stuff published, and if I can get an interview with you..."

She shakes her head. "Not after some rag called me the Jeff Beck of the Chick Guitar. As if that's supposed to be a compliment, like 'not bad, for a girl.' No. I let my guitar speak for herself."

"And screw reporters?" Gabe asks, hopefully.

Without replying, Allie turns to the leftover sorority girl who's standing awkwardly nearby. Allie smiles at her. "Hey... Cindy, right? I've got a 1923 T-Bucket hotrod outside. Wanna see it?"

Angel, her eyes dancing in alcohol-soaked pools, taps Gabe on shoulder. "Come on, cutie, I want to show you something in the kitchen."

Angel leads Gabe out of the living room and into the kitchen, then before Gabe knows what hit him, Angel is kissing him, her tongue dipping down his throat like a plumber's snake.

Suddenly, Gabe is blinded by a white flash.

"Gotcha!" crows the camera-girl. The undeveloped Polaroid picture shoots out, and lands on the floor.

Gabe pulls away from Angel and gapes. "Anna, is that you?"

"Gabe!" the girl replies, smiling broadly.

"I thought that was you. I saw you in the hallway."

Anna snaps a close-up picture of his face. "It's groovy running into you here." She regards him. "What are you doing *here*?" She emphasizes the last word as if he's not cool enough to be hanging with them.

"Well, you probably don't remember when I said I wanted to be a rock and roll journalist. But I am one now. I'm interviewing the band."

"Of course I remember, Gabe! I knew you'd make it big!"

Gabe looks down. "Not exactly big. I need to get an interview with Atom, but he won't talk." He looks at Anna from head to toe; she hasn't changed a bit since the last time he saw her. Still beautiful. "And what are you doing here? You don't still live here, do you? I mean, Sid bought…"

"I'm just hanging out. This is a marathon scene. It's been, what," she looks over at Angel, who is now seated at the table, rolling joints, "five days, now?"

"Time is irrelevant," replies the groupie, spitting a seed.

"Let's go sit in the den," Anna suggests, taking Gabe's hand and leading him from the kitchen.

"Bye, bye, Little Man," Angel calls after them.

The den is even more crowded and reeking of hash than before, if possible. As he and Anna try to find an open seat, Gabe sees that the band have returned from showing off their cars, and they still have their sorority scores at hand. The militant Black girl he'd noticed in the hallway before, Diana, is standing, talking with a geeky, glasses-wearing guy who's basically beige from head-to-toe. Gabe hears the boy saying, "I hear you, sister. My mom's cousin's best friend's neighbor marched in Birmingham."

Gabe has an idea. "Will you excuse me, Anna?"

She nods, and takes a step back.

He steps over to the pair. "Hi, I'm Gabe."

"Diana," says the girl flatly. "And this is Walter."

Walter looks intimidated, even by Gabe. He takes a step back and shoves his hands into the front pockets of his khaki pants.

"I'd like to talk to you," Gabe says, reaching for his notepad.

"You're wasting your time, kid," Diana says with an exasperated sigh. "I was just trying to tell your fellow Caucasian here that I don't date white boys."

"I'm sorry, I think you might have misunderstood my intentions. I don't want to date you." Diana's fierce eyes grow fiercer. "Why not?! You think you're better than me?"

Gabe goes crimson. "No, no. That came out wrong. Look, I'm a journalist. I write about music and, you know, the scene."

Diana crosses her arms. "Oh, so you want to interview me and get the Negro perspective? Get off your white guilt-mobile and find someone else to answer your little questions."

Gabe doesn't think he'd be able to bury himself any deeper if he tried. "Actually, I'm supposed to interview Atom."

"Then why don't you?"

Angel is back, tapping Gabe on the shoulder. "Little Man, I've got something that'll make Atom tell you everything you want to know, and then some."

"What is it?"

"Magic potion."

Mary lowers herself to the ground, and lies flat on the floor, staring at the ceiling.

Walter tries to engage her in conversation. "Hey, Mary Juana. Looking good, girl. Did I tell you I build ham radios? Me and my dad. From scratch, too."

Mary slowly moves her head to look at the geek who is talking to her. She puts her hands up and makes a sign of the cross at him, as if warding off a vampire.

Anna turns to Gabe, laughing. "She kind of reminds me of my mom."

"I was gonna ask you about her. I mean, what the heck happened, I see you one night, then your mom goes off on you, and then you dropped out of school."

Anna sighs. "It's a long story."

"Well, my dad got transferred to Germany a few weeks after we last saw each other." He looks at her sheepishly. "I wrote to you." There's an extended silence. "So, hey, you look great, by the way." He takes her hand and looks at her psychedelic, Day-Glo-bright nails. "Trippy. Are those real?"

"Yeah, thanks."

Angel reaches into her tube-top and her hand comes out full of joints. "Okay, folks, herbs are served!"

Everyone present, even Mary, applauds.

Atom takes his hands off Muffy's knee and sits up. "Angel, be a good girl and hand me a couple doobies."

Angel gives him side-eye. "You wait your turn. The first grass goes to Groovy Nail Girl and Little Man."

Atom lunges forward, taking a joint from Angel. He lights it and draws a huge hit, almost smoking the entire thing in one breath. Then he holds what's left out to Gabe.

He shakes his head. "Even if you won't talk to me, I'm supposed to be working here, getting interviews. Maybe I should stay straight."

"You can interview me, if you want," Anna says shyly.

"Um, okay," he says, pulling the notebook and a pencil from his pocket.

Anna rests her head on his shoulder. "So, what do you want to ask me?"

What don't I want to ask you? "Tell me about your nails, the design."

Angel leans over to inspect them. "Yeah, how do you get that far-out shine to your nails?"

Anna looks at her own nails. "It's this weird polish I found." Anna pulls out a vial of nail varnish that looks like the chemical blue of a Tidy Bowl toilet.

Angel reaches for it. "Can I see it?"

"Yeah, but be careful. I have to dilute it, one part lacquer to two parts water, because it's so strong. And it's seriously toxic. You can only find it on the black market and the woman who sold it to me said that one speck of it, if put right on your skin, could singe it, and if you drank that speck, you'd probably die. She also said she was a witch, but she just looked like an old lady to me."

"A witch, huh?" Angel asks, handing the bottle back to Anna, who pockets it.

Gabe says, "But why would you want to put all that deadly stuff on your fingernails?"

"Besides the fact that this stuff makes my nails look cooler than anyone else's? Well, I guess I like the contrast between beauty and danger."

Gabe scribbles something down. "Beauty and danger, I like that, Anna."

"This reminds me of *The Diabolical Dr. Z*," says Angel.

Gabe looks puzzled.

"A movie," Angel clarifies. "About a murderous woman with poison fingernails. I was a film student before I dropped out to hang with the bands."

"I'd like to interview you, too," Gabe says.

Micro-Dot shrugs, then says to Angel-Dust, "Poison on our fingernails would certainly keep the guys in line."

Gabe sits back, watching the party, smiling, taking the whole scene in.

Ziggy starts a drumbeat with his hands slapping his thighs, Allie plucks out some notes on her guitar, and Atom gets up and goes over to the piano. He removes a tuning fork from his back pocket and hits it against his knee to test the tone. They play an impromptu cover of *Witchy Woman*, to the low-key delight of the cannabis-infused crowd. As the song reaches its final notes, Anna snaps a shot of Atom at the piano, smiling broadly.

"Look," she says, holding the developing photo out to Gabe. "A spirit."

Gabe squints. "Where?" He watches as Atom's form comes into focus. He thinks he sees a dark shape sitting next to Atom, but as the image gets sharper and more colorful, the blotch fades.

"Never mind," Anna says, walking away from him and into the crowd. "Catch you later."

Gabe puts the photo into his jacket pocket, then turns his attention to Angel and Dot. "Hey, ladies, would you mind if I ask for just a few minutes of your time for an interview?"

"Why?" asks Dot.

"I'm trying to get a feel for the band, why people dig them, you know?"

The groupies nod, and Gabe suggests they go into the kitchen, where it's somewhat quieter. Gabe, Dot, and Angel sit down at the kitchen table. There's a long silence. Gabe isn't sure how to begin.

Angel says, "So, what do you want to ask us, Little Man?"

"I guess for starters, how did you two become, group… or I mean, how did you two come to follow the band?"

Dot grins. "You mean, how long have we been *groupies*? Isn't that what you wanted to say?"

Gabe takes out his notebook and poises his pencil. "Yeah."

Angel turns to her friend. "Hey, Micro-Dot, can you get me a measuring cup?"

Dot goes to a kitchen shelf to retrieve a huge, oversized cup. From underneath the table, Angel takes out a big spoon and a can of a flour-like substance.

Gabe's eyes widen. "Is that cocaine?"

Dot guffaws. "No."

"What is it then?"

Dot gives Angel a conspiratorial look. "Should we tell him?"

Angel asks Gabe, "When are you running your story?"

"Well," Gabe admits, "I don't have it sold yet."

"Okay," Angel says, "you can put what we're doing on the record, but you can't say anything about this to anyone right now. We're Plaster Casters."

Gabe remembered hearing about the special clique of groupies who make molds of group members' members. They were planning on opening a museum and putting rock star's cock-casts on display like works of art. He didn't think it was true, though.

...

"Okay, thanks," Gabe mutters, stuffing his notepad back into his pocket.

"Get Groovy Nail Girl back, and you'll have the exclusive photo of Atom's cast," Dot promises, winking.

Gabe gets up and heads for the den. No one's there except for Mary, who is staring at her hands as if she's never seen them before. He continues following the sounds of the party, which has moved from inside to late afternoon sunshine.

Along with the hippies and squares are three new guests—biker-types wearing leather cuts with the words "Sons of Chagrin" embroidered on the back.

Gabe sidles up to Atom. "Who are they?"

Atom shrugs. He's put a shirt on now, a thin, billowy one with long poet-style sleeves "Friends of Sid's, I guess."

"Hm. Well, have you seen Anna? She kind of disappeared on me."

Atom shakes his head, then addresses the crowd. "Has anyone seen the girl with the camera and fingernails?"

People shake their heads and murmur, but one of the bikers stands and says, "Ooh-fucking-la-la, do I like broads with nails. And a camera, too, huh?" He's well over 6-foot tall, his brawny arms are covered in badly-drawn tattoos, and he has a heavy, almost cartoonish, French accent. "Kinky little thing."

Atom shakes his head. "Whoa, whoa, peace, dudes. Anna's underage. And she's Sid's friend, so hands off."

The biker echoes, "Sid?" He pronounces it like "seed."

Atom frowns. "The guy you said you knew; the one who invited you to the party."

Gabe is intrigued by the new guests. And somewhat terrified of them, too. The other two—a scrawny Latino, and a stout, bald, albino—are equally scary, but they seem to be deferring to the French guy. He must be the leader. Gabe decides to interview him.

"Hey, man," he says, offering his hand. "I'm Gabe. I'm a reporter."

The three men laugh, revealing discolored teeth, and in the alpha's case, a gold-plated cap. "I'm Rubber," he says. "This is Necro," he indicates the skinny fellow. "And this is Spooky." The chunky man raises a pair of well-worn nunchakus in greeting. "You seem pretty young for a reporter. You want to interview us?" Rubber takes a flask out of the inner pocket of his leather jacket. He downs a big gulp.

Atom steps over. "Whatcha got there?"

Rubber licks his lips. "Manitoba Moonshine." He passes the flask to the singer.

Atom takes a small sip and chokes. He leans forward as if to let out all the air and extinguish the fire raging in his body. "Got... quite... a kick," he wheezes.

Rubber laughs, then he grabs the flask back and takes a swig. "Some people say this shit'll kill you." Rubber offers the flask again, but Atom waves it off. Anger blazes in Rubber's dark eyes. "You fucking prick! *Freres* drink together."

Atom sputters, "Alright, dude, I'm hip, *frère. Frere Jacques.*"

Gabe sees his chance. "Now that you're so loose, Atom, maybe you can relax some more with a no-stress interview?"

Atom shakes his head and smiles. "You never give up, do you?"

Gabe mutters, "Sorry."

Atom grins. "No, you're not, and I like that. Hustling. You're alright, Little Man. Go get some more interviews."

Gabe takes a few steps away, but stays within earshot. Allie, carrying her guitar in its case, announces that she's going home to finish the song she and Ziggy have been working on.

Ziggy stands. "Good idea. This party's lame, anyway." Blair glares at him. "Later," Ziggy says, following his bandmate through a side-gate.

There goes my hope of interviewing the band, Gabe thinks. *I'm going to have to work extra hard on Atom.*

As Rubber and Atom talk, Gabe sees Necro and Spooky go inside the house. Should he follow them to get a few quotes? Just as he's debating, Gabe feels an elbow in his ribs. It's Angel. "Hey, Little Man," she smirks, "Ask Rubber how he got his name. That's quite a story."

"You know him?" Gabe asks, taken aback. The ethereal girl doesn't seem like the biker-loving type.

"Never saw him before today. But did I get an eyeful when I accidentally walked in on him in the bathroom." She stretches her arms as wide as they'll go.

"Um, well... I'm not writing that kind of article. It's all about the music."

"I tell ya, that thing'd make anyone sing."

Rubber ambles over, arms crossed. "Are you talking about me? I heard someone say my name."

Gabe feels put on the spot by Angel, but he's got nothing—and nothing to lose. "Rubber, can I get a quick interview with you?"

Rubber downs the rest of the contents of his flask, then lights an unfiltered cigarette. "Sweet *merde* of God, I got stories, little fucker. Bend over and I'll drive."

Gabe's jaw drops. "What?"

"I'm gonna talk; you just shut up and write." Rubber sits down next to Gabe. "Let's start with the first time I had to punk a guy's ass. I was nine, and living in Montreal. By myself."

"By yourself? Where were your parents?"

"They kicked it. Just leave it at that."

"Okay, so you came down from Canada—and that's kind of ironic because it seems like all the guys here want to go *to* Canada to avoid the draft."

"Pansies! I'd love to join the army *Americain* so I can go kick some Chinamen's asses, y'know?"

"But they're Viet Cong."

"But those army fucks won't take me just 'cause I done some time in Alcatraz. So, then I met up with my boys, Spooky and Necro, and then we hit the road on our choppers and..."

Gabe writes as quickly as he can, but he can't keep up. His notes are a jumble of phrases including "prison wife," "spork shank," and "backdoor parole."

In the periphery of his vision, Gabe catches a camera flash. *Anna's back!* Gabe interrupts Rubber, "Do you mind if we take a break? I need to talk to Anna."

Rubber glances over the strawberry blonde, then waves the boy away. "Go ahead, talk to your little girl now." He leers at Anna. "I'll talk to her later."

Gabe goes to Anna and taps her on the shoulder. "I'm so glad you came back."

Anna smiles, but she looks sad. "I always come back."

Rubber sweeps by the pair, on his way inside the house.

"Who's that guy?" Anna asks. "Is Sid home yet?"

"No, I haven't seen Sid since he left," Gabe lowers his voice, "on a drug run. Apparently, he invited that guy. Rubber is his name."

Rubber brushes past again, now on his way back to the courtyard. He's carrying two full bottles of Jack Daniels, one in each hand.

He sits down next to Atom and Angel. Atom calls out to Gabe and Anna. "Hey Gabe! And hey, you, um..."

"Groovy Nail Girl," Angel supplies.

They're sitting in a semi-circle, passing the bottles around, plus a bong. Gabe doesn't partake. Instead, he takes notes. As the afternoon fades into evening, the rest of the guests trickle out the side gate, leaving only Gabe, Anna, Atom, the three groupies, and three bikers.

Atom says, "You know, Rubber, I'm something of a biker myself. I used to love cruising around on my Kawasaki. Up through Mulholland Drive, down into the Valley."

Rubber guffaws. "Kawasaki! That's a child's bike." He spits. "When one reaches manhood, one wants a real man's ride: a Harley. I've gone from one end of Pacific Coast Highway to the other in a single shot going over 144 kilometers per hour."

"I see what you mean," says Atom. "But when I needed more speed, I got myself a sports car."

"That's alright for you, I guess, but me, I'd feel like a pussy fenced inside the safety of a *voiture*—an automobile. I'm more the... how you say, *adventurous* sort."

"That does sound adventurous, riding up and down the coast."

Rubber looks pleased.

Atom adds, "Of course, me and my band are going on tour all over the country, and next year, probably all over the world."

Rubber sneers. "You say you're in some band, or something?"

Angel's eyes light up, and not just from her righteous buzz. "You didn't know? He's in The Near-Death Experience."

Rubber crosses his arms. "Near Death? Never heard of them. Do you play something?"

Atom sits up straighter. "I'm the lead singer. And main songwriter." Atom takes his tuning fork out from his back pocket and hits it against Angel's head. "You're in tune, Angel."

Rubber looks bored. "So you don't play anything, do you?"

"A little guitar, some piano."

Rubber gives a saccharin smile, the gold tooth glinting in the waning sun. "Cute. I used to work security for The Rolling Stones. Now *that's* a motherfuckin' band. We'd be on stage at stadiums. Ever look fifty thousand people in the face?"

Atom tenses. "Well, not yet, but you know, it's not about the size of the audience—"

"Don't bullshit me and tell me size don't matter—like it's not the meat, it's the motion. Take it from a pro, son: it's the meat."

"You talk a good game."

Angel pipes up. "It's not all talk."

Rubber nods. "And when I play my kind of games, I win."

It's clear to Gabe that Rubber is really getting under Atom's skin. He writes this observation down.

"Alright, then, Rubber," Atom says. "Show the rest of us why they call you that."

Rubber stands. "*Tres bon.*" He laughs. "But I'm telling you, if you try sucking on it, you'll have your own near-death experience."

Atom rolls his eyes. "Ha. Funny. I already had a near-death experience, almost drowning in the Pacific while surfing; that's how come I named the band that."

Rubber snorts. "Nearly dying only *once*? If you live life as a man, as I do, you'll be on death's door every day. Popping bennies, drinking a keg, and cranking full throttle down the canyon with the Grim Reaper holding on for dear life. Don't take your foot off the gas until you hear glass breaking. There's your near-death experience!"

"Okay, enough talk." Atom makes a gesture of impatience. "Let's see this thing."

Rubber grins toothily, making him look like a crocodile. "Back in the joint I'd never show it to another man unless he begs. But what the hell." The biker slowly, teasingly, unzips his pants. He shakes his hips as he unveils his credentials.

There's a drawn-out silence while the others present take in the enormity of the thing. Angel and Dot applaud. Gabe and Anna both shield their eyes with their hands, as if they're trying not to look directly into the sun. Atom's eyes are round as saucers. Rubber stands proudly, large, calloused hands on his bare hips.

As they stare, a sharp scream comes from inside the house.

Rubber stuffs himself back in, while Atom and Gabe, followed by the girls, rush to see what the commotion is about. Spooky and Necro have bound Mary's hands with one of their belts and propped her against the wall with an apple on her head. Spooky has a pocket knife poised in the air, ready to try and spear the fruit from a distance. Mary is crying, but she's too wasted to move or try to get away.

Atom rushes forward and pushes Spooky away, knocking the knife out of the biker's hand. "Stay away from that girl."

Just then, Rubber comes bounding in. "Don't you be touching my boys."

Atom snaps, "Your boys are fucking with my girls."

"If you're fucking with my boys, you're fucking with me."

Spooky is unimpressed. He sharpens the knife on his teeth, and sparks fly from the blade. Necro starts swinging his nunchakus so fast, the air whistles.

The atmosphere is thick with tension. Gabe takes a few steps back, then starts writing down what he's seeing.

Atom looks around the room, just realizing that everyone else has gone. There's no one here to help him. He turns back to the head biker. "You'd better leave."

Rubber snickers. "A real man would make me."

Atom gets into a fight-stance, making fists. "If that's how you want it." He dips his head toward the three groupies, and Gabe and Anna. "Clear the room."

Rubber sneers. "You heard him. This ain't a sight for ladies. You gals, and I include that little pansy reporter over there, better *sortez*. I always eliminate witnesses. Va!"

The groupies and young couple back into the hallway, but they can still see what's going on.

Necro drops his nunchakus to the ground and grabs Atom's arms, pinning them behind his back. Spooky approaches, wielding his small but sharp knife.

Rubber holds up a hand. "Stop, *mons garcons*. He's mine."

"No!" Angel yells.

Rubber snaps, "Necro, Spooky—shut them up!"

Necro lets go of Atom, stoops to grab his weapon from the shag carpet, then heads for the trembling bystanders. Spooky is right behind him. They're quickly hustled into the kitchen. Gabe cowers with the rest, listening to the commotion going on in the den as the two bikers block the doorway.

The sounds of a scuffle fill the air.

Then abruptly...

...an eerie silence.

Rubber calls sweetly, "Yoo-hoo, Angel-Dust! Rubber's gettin' all freshed up for you, 'cause you're gonna be my first gal, *numbre un*. And bring me one of your mixed drinks I've heard so much about."

Necro and Spooky chuckle, and step aside.

Angel stays where she is, clearly thinking about what to do. Then she turns and goes to the kitchen table, where she left the white powder. "Rubber's going to love this," she announces to the room.

Necro and Spooky look at the bag of power.

"Yes, he will," Necro says. "I once saw him snort a whole bowlful of PCP mixed with broken glass."

Anna says, "I have something for that, Angel. A special ingredient." She glances pointedly at her fingernails.

Smart, Gabe thinks.

"I'll get the water," Dot says, moving over to the sink. She picks up a glass and fills it.

Rubber calls out again. "Angel, come over and get your ride on the Von Zeppelin!"

Gabe follows the girls out of the kitchen, with the bikers so close on him he can feel the heat of their whisky-reeking breaths behind him.

Rubber is sitting on the red velvet couch, his arms sprawled out like a king enjoying his throne. Lying on the floor at his feet is Atom, face-up, with his own tuning fork protruding from one eye. Blood trickles from his mouth, and his body is eerily still.

Gabe gasps, and Anna takes his hand. Dot leans in and whispers, "Shhh."

The boy watches as Angel dumps some of the powder into the large glass of water. Then Anna sidles closer, taking the bottle of nail polish from her back pocket. She dumps the contents into the mix.

"What is this?" Rubber asks, half-standing. "That's not a drink."

"You're right, it's Plaster of Paris."

Rubber frowns. "I hate that shit, my mom used to make me eat it, before I kicked her ass."

"No, silly, it's for your cock—the most amazing, astounding, alluring, and everything else that starts with an A and ends with a G. Have you heard of The Plaster Casters?"

Rubber squints. "You're gonna put this on The Blimp?"

"We think something as magnificent as that should be immortalized for all of eternity."

Angel steps over Atom's body, gingerly. Then

she reaches down and unzips Rubber's pants, freeing his beast.

Rubber sighs and settles back. He shuts his eyes. "If you think you got enough plaster, then lay it on me, *cherie*."

Angel dumps the bubbling blue contents from the glass, directly onto Rubber's exposed appendage.

The chemical hits his flesh and sizzles.

"*Mon* fucking *dieu!*" the biker bleats, scrambling to his feet. He trips over Atom's body, flopping back into the cushions. "Holy *merde*, I'm burning!"

The plaster mix expands and grows, engulfing Rubber's midsection. It takes shape, shooting down to his legs and jetting up his chest and over his face. The biker is nothing but a massive blue blob.

Gabe sees Spooky and Necro running toward the front door, then he hears it slam, followed by the roar of motorcycles starting up, then peeling away.

Speaking of peeling away... Gabe thinks perversely, watching as Rubber's clothes and flesh dissolves. Gabe sees a flash of skeleton and skull, then there's nothing left but a vivid indigo stain.

"Where did he go?" Gabe gasps, turning to Anna. "What's in that polish?"

Anna is standing there, smiling... and dissolving. Not like Rubber, it's more of a fade, like the reverse of a Polaroid developing. And then she, too, is gone.

"Wha—?" Gabe looks at Angel, Dot, and Mary, wide-eyed.

"She's at peace," whispers Angel.

Gabe thinks he knows why he never saw Anna after that night when they were 14. Why she didn't look any different tonight. "She's... a ghost?"

Dot nods. "*Was.* Sid says she was here when he moved in. Not moaning or scaring people; just appearing out of nowhere with a camera in her hand."

"You know, like tonight," says Angel.

Dot continues, "The owner before Sid was some crazy lady who murdered her daughter by hacking her to pieces. To this day, the cops can't find all of the girl's body parts but they think they're buried somewhere on this property.

"Oh, shit," Gabe says.

"You can say that again!" It's Atom, sitting up and yanking the fork from his eye. The utensil carries bits of his eyeball on its tines, but he's unfazed. He's probably taken enough drugs tonight to tranquilize a pachyderm, but tomorrow it's gonna hurt like hell. The singer takes a gander at what's left of Rubber. "I know this shithead had to go, but don't you girls think that what you did was a little extreme?"

Angel shrugs. Dot makes a face.

"I'm just glad it wasn't *me*," says Mary. "That biker could have missed the apple on my head. I might have wound up like you." She winks at him.

"Yeah, I saved you," Atom grouses, "only to wind up like this." He points to his face.

"I'd still do you," Angel says with a suggestive smirk.

Somehow through the shock of all this, Gabe hears the front door open and close.

It's Sid, holding a small brown paper bag. "Here comes the peyote man!" he calls out cheerily. He steps into the den and stops dead in his tracks as he takes in the new turn of events.

Sid screams "What the motherfucking fuck?" a dozen times and hurls some used party plates and glasses against the wall, which is filled with framed gold records. A few of them slide to the shaggy carpeted floor.

Once Sid's got that out of his system, he starts to pace, all the while addressing the rest who are still gathered there, cowering. "Okay, no one says shit about this. Everybody got that? We don't want the fuzz here looking for drugs or runaway teens, do we, girls?"

The groupies flip him off. Sid ought to know that they'd sooner be victims of the Boston Strangler than ever call the fucking pigs.

Sid's anger turns to Atom. "And you! What do you think's gonna happen if RCA finds out the cops are asking you questions about what went down here?"

"I get it, Sid. I'll be dropped by the label and the tour will be kaput," says Atom. He stops to daub some fluid that has accumulated in what was left of his right eye with his sleeve. "It doesn't matter, man. I'm done. I'm out. I mean, look at me."

Atom's got a point, thinks Gabe. *Ray Charles, Stevie Wonder, those blind dudes are cool, but who's going to pay to see this eye oozing Cyclops on stage?*

"Oh, quit your blubbering," Sid tells Atom. "Don't worry, I know Sammy Davis, Jr.'s glass man. The doc can blow you a new eye in about an hour."

"And we can blow you while you wait," Angel tells Atom. The other girls nod.

Atom seems genuinely touched by their gesture, or rather, their promised gestures. He gives Dot, Angel, and Mary hugs.

Gabe decides that this is a good time to jet so he turns toward the door. He's about to twist the door handle when Sid yells, "Where the fuck do you think *you're* going, kid?!"

Gabe stops in his tracks, stammering that he didn't get any quotes for the record so he wouldn't be using any names or anything for his article, so can he please go?

"Not only are you not gonna use names, champ," Sid continues, "But this whole party never happened. You better not write dick about what you saw tonight."

To Gabe, that is too much. He takes his journalism seriously. "No. I came here tonight to see and then write about I saw here," he says, "And that's exactly what I'm going to do." He surprises himself with his newfound courage.

Sid tries a different tactic. "Okay, sport," he says, smiling obsequiously at Gabe. "I can see you're a professional little fellow. Tell you what: forget about writing about tonight. You meet me over at Capitol Records tomorrow and we'll set you up with an interview with Russell Aquarius."

Sid adds that if anyone finds out that Rubber died here, his cohorts "are gonna come back and they're not only gonna be looking for me, they're gonna look for you, too. I'll have no choice but to tell them where to find you."

That settles it for Gabe. The last thing he needs is trouble from those violent and crazy Canucks. He tells the group that his lips are sealed, bids them all adieu, and promises Sid he'll be there the following night for a sit-down with Russell.

"Oh, and Atom," Gabe adds, "instead of a glass eye, you might want to think about getting an eye patch. My Uncle Dick's got one and the ladies he scores with love it."

Sid laughs sarcastically and ushers Gabe out the door. "Eye patches are for assholes."

The door shuts, and Gabe turns around. He sees his face in the mirror—older and wiser somehow, but still in need of longer sideburns. He gazes deep into the glass, hoping to see Anna one last time, but she is gone.

Gabe gets on his bike and pedals into the dark on his journey home.

Other than the violence, the ghosts, and douchebags like Sid, he thinks, *I'm really starting to dig the music biz.*

Daydream Bereaver
Shane Bitterling

As the *Beach Bonkers* film crew set up before dawn for the first shot, they found the head of Slim hanging 10 on the end of his surfboard. Chalked up to a shark attack, it had washed ashore sometime early in the morning and was completely forgotten about by noon. Johnny Duke stammered a makeshift eulogy as the coroner wheeled away with it in a small cooler. Slim was the bassist, and this was the best sendoff one of those could hope for.

Patty cooed her condolences to Johnny, wriggling in her bikini and lightly pawing at his chest. He lowered his shades and checked her from painted toes to brunette tip. He took her hand and spun her around.

"It's fine, chickie. You're a knockout," he said. Her face wrinkled. He had other things on his mind besides Slim. But at least she had his attention. "I gotta go practice this bit, but stay close. I've got big plans for you later." He strutted towards the director, who was talking with Magilla, Joe and a beach bum kid they pulled off the sand and would be standing in for Slim.

Patty watched as Johnny huddled with the boys. Magilla cocked his head to look past Johnny. His smile turned to a sigh when he saw Patty there. The others tried to make their quick gaze less obvious, which made it more obvious they were talking about her. Joe pivoted. The new kid waved at her. The director did a full turn, then stared directly into the sun before nodding and blinking his approval to Johnny.

She quickly snapped the elastic of her bikini bottom with her thumbs then hoisted her breasts from underneath to adjust her top. Then she posed as if nobody were watching. And they weren't anymore. Johnny had missed it. But she had been noticed. By nighttime, Johnny would be hers and hers forever and ever. She'd dreamed of this moment for two years. A dream that was all-consuming ever since she spotted that first record at the Ben Franklin. It was that cover that got her. Johnny's pouty lips she wanted to smooch. Those piercing blue eyes she wanted to gaze into. That slicked back duck-butt hair she wanted to muss as those pouty lips nibbled on her neck. She didn't listen to the record for days. She just stared at the cover. And it stared back. The seven-inch by seven-inch photo guarded her from the nightstand as she slept. It watched her as she ate her Malt-O-Meal in the morning. It watched her tinkle.

When she was fully smitten, she finally listened to the wax. She was afraid the voice wouldn't live up to her expectations. But it did. Her friends hated it and thought he sounded like a goober. "A no-talent phony bologna wannabe with a voice that couldn't carry a tune in a bucket the size of Des Moines," Deb said. Patty hadn't talked to Deb since. Deb was jealous and Patty wouldn't stand for anybody talking about her man like that. "Man, he doesn't even know you exist. This is unhealthy."

"Eating that Zagnut isn't healthy, Deb," Patty said to the sand she now stood on. But Deb was right. That single was the only one that Johnny Duke would ever release. *Surf You Up* was a modest hit on local stations, but never broke out across the country. There was some controversy about whether Johnny actually sang it at all. What wasn't up for debate was that his uncle owned radio stations and was now venturing into movies.

When Patty heard about the contest to win a walk-on part for *Beach Bonkers* on the radio, she had to change her underwear. She called out sick from school for four days straight, waiting for that moment. And then that moment came. She felt in her bones that this would have been the day, but when the disc jockey opened the phone lines to the tenth caller, her brain refused to send the appropriate directions to dial the phone. She stared at it and pointed with her forefinger, but couldn't make the necessary half step to actually touch the phone. She willed herself to fall forward, her finger planting itself in the dial. Grease finally lubed her brain wheels and like lightning, she was able to call the station.

"I won! I won! I won! Oh, Johnny, baby, we'll finally be together!"

"Is this about the contest?" the station's secretary said.

It was, and Patty asked where she should show up to claim her prize and when. If she got some kind of certificate or if she should wait for Johnny to call her. "And what should I wear?"

"I'm sorry," the secretary said. "That prize was won by a Doris Feinstein several minutes ago. Didn't you hear it over the airwaves? That contest is over. Lucky gal, that Doris Feinstein."

Patty stood silent. Her lips quivering. Eyes twitching. "Doris Feinstein," she repeated. And she hung up the phone. Picked it up again, then slammed it down for maximum satisfaction.

Instead of experiencing a forever memory, Doris Feinstein woke up to total disappointment when she discovered all the tires on her car had been slashed.

Nobody was going to tell Patty she was a loser on a technicality. And nobody was going to get in the way of her and Johnny's love.

"Chickie," Johnny said, breaking her reverie. "Scoot on over and see what we're doing. You're gonna be in this scene."

This was her moment. She jogged, dragging the tips of her toes in the sand with each long-legged stride. The director put his arm around her shoulder and guided her to where he wanted her to stand. She didn't like other men touching her and looked to Johnny to punch him in the snotbox. He didn't read her well, but she could fix this over time.

In the scene, Johnny would be crooning to a lovely beachgoer, and that beachgoer was going to be Patty. The Earls would all be there, helping him serenade her, as if he needed any help.

The scene was blocked and the director yelled, "Action!" A man nearby placed a needle on the record and the song emanated from speakers. Joe pretended to play his guitar along with the recording. The kid wasn't sure how to hold his bass so bit his lip and jiggled it around. Magilla slapped his congas in time with the song and the director yelled, "Cut."

Magilla was told multiple times that he wasn't actually playing because it would mess up the sound for the picture. He kept arguing that it wouldn't come off as real if he didn't smack those skins like they deserved. He wasn't a phony, and refused to pretend to be one.

"But you're really going to sing to me, right?" Patty asked.

Johnny looked at her pouting lips and felt her light pawing at his bare chest. He gulped. "Of course I am, chickie." Johnny demanded that this time, they would play for real. They'd just fix it all in post-production. The director tossed the script pages over his head and told them to do whatever they wanted. He was using a pseudonym on this turkey anyway.

Action was called and Magilla worked the congas into a sensuous frenzy. A riff on what he played the night before. The crew were silently snapping their fingers. Joe joined in, adding a few flares not on the recording. The kid bobbed his head and turned away from the camera in embarrassment. Johnny strutted around Patty like a rooster, singing off-key, but she didn't notice. It was the most beautiful thing she'd ever heard. He was singing his song directly to *her*. Their song.

Her knees were jelly, but she knew if she fell, it would break the intense eye contact she had with him.

Even the ocean seemed to be in step with the sounds of the band. A tide swelled high, casting a shadow on the crew, and crashed violently on the beach. Then dissipated as quickly as it came.

The director saw the girl in frame, behind the band. Staring. Swaying her hips to the music in an unnatural way. Almost serpentine. He hadn't noticed her entering the shot from left or right. The wave dashed and she was just there. "Cut! She's in the shot. Get her out of the shot!"

The Earls stopped. All eyes turned to her. Her swaying abruptly ended and she marched towards them, arms akimbo.

"What a bee-you-tee," Johnny said. Patty was quick with a slug to the stomach for that, which doubled him over. But the girl was a beauty. Her shimmering seaweed bikini showed off a perfect, toned and tight body with deadman's curves any beach boy would happily careen through the guardrail for. Chiseled cheekbones, accentuating her full lips and exotic, large, green eyes that were dazzling and hypnotic. Her perfect features capped off with a glorious, raven black beehive hairdo that came down and covered her ears with a bob.

The men gawked with their mouths hanging wide. Magilla dropped his sticks in the sand and Joe pulled at his guitar strap around his shoulder.

Patty thought she looked like a tramp. Or Italian. She noticed something that looked like a crab claw receding into the center of the girl's beehive and covering its tracks with her hair as she bounced with purpose towards them. She snorted at the thought of a crab emerging from her hair and pinching one of the boy's noses when they tried to swap spit with her. But not Johnny. He only had eyes for Patty. He would never do that to her.

The girl stood before them. She mesmerized them all with her intense gaze, rendering the men silent, but tongues wagging. "Where is it?" the girl said.

"Where is what?" Johnny asked, pulling himself together.

"Your mating call? I have come," she said.

The beach bum kid inadvertently whistled through his gapped teeth.

"Mating call? You mean our tunes," Johnny said.

"Tuna?" she asked. Then licked her lips.

Johnny took her by the shoulders and guided her front and center. He looked to the director, who was shaking his head, a cigarette dangling incredulously from his lips.

Johnny gave the scene a once-over. Patty smiled as he took her by the hand. Then guided her several yards camera left. He looked to the director again, who nodded.

"Can you dance, chickie?" Johnny asked the girl. She stared at his neckline.

"I can dance. I dance real good," Patty said from the sidelines.

The director called, "Action," and Johnny counted it down. The Earls played like their lives depended on it. Even the beach bum kid was able to stutter out a chord here and there. The rhythm made her gyrate the likes of which none of the men had ever witnessed. Undulating as if her bones were fluid. Never taking her eyes off of Johnny, who sang better than he ever had in his life.

She squirmed around Johnny's body to Magilla's beat as if they had rehearsed this for weeks.

The director beamed and said to the cameraman, "This is the scene that will get me out of this sandy shitbox forever. The studios are gonna love me. The *real* studios."

Patty danced in her now-unspectacular way. She inched herself into the side of the frame, glaring at Johnny and motioning him to join her. Johnny didn't notice her. But the director did. He whispered to an assistant, who then pulled Patty out of frame by her bikini strap.

The mystery girl placed her hands on either side of Johnny's face. He winced at the touch, but never sang off key. Her body was still roiling like the ocean itself. "Mate with me."

Johnny's eyes widened. He knew he would never get another take like this, so he soldiered on with the song. Vicelike, she held his head tightly. Gold shimmered deep within her green eyes. Electric pain darted across his face and down his neck. Her beehive slowly began to unravel. "I will have you for dinner."

The song ended abruptly, and finally, for Johnny. Her dance ended on the last conga beat. The thing in her hair retreated once more. The crew was abuzz with activity. She still held him tight, glaring at him. He couldn't look away.

"I don't know how to get another angle of that. It'll never happen again," the director said, throwing his hat to the sand.

Patty ran to Johnny, who was still trancing out. "Can I have a word with you?"

"Sure," he said, in a haze.

"Alone," Patty said. Neither Johnny nor the girl relinquished their gaze. "Johnny's with me!"

Patty grabbed the girl by the arms and forced her hands from Johnny's face. The girl turned on her, mouth widening to severe widths and hissed from the deepest depths of her belly, which made her nose wrinkle. In that moment, Patty would swear the girl had multiple rows of teeth going all the way down to where a lady should never let a man look.

"And by the way, you smell like a can of spoiled Starkist."

Johnny rubbed the sides of his face, where red, round welts had grown where the girl had her hands. He was sweating profusely and smiling. Patty knew that look. Her father had the same one when she accidentally walked in on her parents one time during a thunderstorm when she was eight.

"Come here, you." Patty dragged Johnny away from the set. "Why, Johnny?" Johnny looked over his shoulder at the girl, who was burning a hole into Patty with her hellish glare. Patty grabbed him by the sides of his face and forced him to look her in the eye.

The director threw up his arms and announced that they'd pick it up tomorrow. They got enough gold on film today, that if they only released that scene, he would be in the catbird seat.

"Yikeys," Johnny said as the welts burned under Patty's touch.

"What's the deal, baby? I thought we had something special, you and me," she said.

"I dunno, chickie. I'm not sure what happened along the way," he said as he tried to turn back to the girl, but was again forced to look at Patty. "I guess things just didn't work out between us."

"But all that time we had together. The song you sang to me. That was for me."

"Well, to be honest…"

"It was for me, Johnny. Not that bimbo. Or any other bimbo. Get me?" She shook him by the face. He winced.

"Whatever you say. Just stop paining my face, please."

Patty let him go. Kissed her middle and forefingers and placed them on each of Johnny's cheeks. "There, there. Patty gonna make her man all better."

Johnny forced a smile and slowly backed away. "I gotta take care of some stuff before everybody bolts. I'll catch you on the flip-flop?" He couldn't wait to talk to the director and have her banned from the set. If he had his way, she wouldn't even be allowed to watch the picture when it came out. Any other day, Patty would be a great notch on his belt. But she was nothing compared to the girl with green eyes and those impossible hips.

"You mean the party on the beach tonight, right?" Patty said.

"You know about that?"

"I heard the boys talking about it earlier. That's what you mean, right? Hanging out with you by the bonfire. Right?"

"I'm probably not going to make it. Definitely not making it," he said. At least not now. He hoped to be making it with the green-eyed girl. She wanted to mate. He'd just have to find another place for it.

"I'm making you supper. You've worked so hard all day. You need to eat and keep up your manly strength. You like fish, right?"

"Why do all you goofy girls wanna cook for me all of a sudden?"

"I read you liked fish in *Teeny Bopper* magazine, silly. I'll find you," Patty said as she skipped over the sand.

"Of course you will. Shit."

...

As evening swallowed the last of the sun, Magilla's bonfire lit up the beach. Joe and a select few members of the crew roasted marshmallows, drank beers, and relaxed.

Patty was there, hunting for Johnny. Magilla relayed the message that Johnny wasn't feeling well and had to bail on the party. Patty glared at him as if it were his fault. "You may as well just go home," Magilla said with a sly wink to Joe. "Or you can hang out with me for the night. Maybe get to know each other better."

"As if," Patty said and kicked up sand as she stomped away.

Patty stomped around a nearby alcove, racking her brain. "Wherever are you, Johnny? You said you'd be here tonight. It's our first real date. I was going to make you dinner. Not a good way to start a life together, Johnathan."

She heard something nearby, on the other side of the rocks. A gasping whistle and stuttering. Then a nervous giggle.

Patty shimmied on her belly over the crest of rocks and looked down. From high, a small bonfire alighted the girl straddling an unseen man who was pinned down on the sand floor. "Mate with me," the girl said.

"Johnny!" Patty whispered. "How could you?"

The bodies shifted and Patty could make out that the man was not Johnny, but the pimply-faced beach bum she saw fiddling with a guitar earlier. He was squirming under the girl, who was stronger than she looked.

"Shouldn't I buy you a soda pop or something first?" the kid said as he struggled.

Magilla's conga beat traveled over the sand, shore and stone and finally reached them. The girl began grinding to the beat. The kid yelped and hooted with his pants around his ankles. The girl's grip on his body was unbreakable.

Accompanying Magilla's beat was Johnny's voice, crooning over the breeze. He showed up to be with Patty, or so she thought. But Johnny would have to wait. The show below was too good to miss.

Patty saw the beehive rocking with the rhythm. It started to unravel. No. It was unraveling itself. Strands of hair unwound and gathered in the back. The crablike thing appeared from impossibly deep within the girl's head. It clamped and pinched at the night air. It was hard to tell if the boy was in agony or ecstasy. A virginal lover or a bleating lamb. The girl reared her head back and opened her mouth. Wider and wider still. Patty heard as the girl's jaws unhinged, creating a cavernous maw filled with never-ending rows of teeth.

Patty gasped. The girl looked dead into her eyes. A grotesque smile formed at her separated lips. Like a snake striking, the girl bit down on the kid's head, swallowing it whole. Blood splattered black across the moonlit sand.

Patty screamed and turned to run. To warn the others. No. Just Johnny. He would be the father of their many children. Her feet slipped on the night slick rocks. She lost her footing and fell into the alcove, on top of the headless beach bum.

She scampered to her feet. Looked for a way out. A way back to Johnny. The blood from the kid had ruined her dress. She kicked his body, then apologized. A sound behind her. She turned to face the gaping maw of the girl.

"I knew you smelled like a fishy one," Patty said as the girl, all mouth, legs, and arms, forced her back against the rocks. Patty grabbed at the girl's neck, under the bob, but its slickness wouldn't allow her a handhold. Her fingers slipped inside a fold on the neck and touched wet meat. She felt that sensation before. Gills.

Patty yanked and the girl bellowed. She took the opportunity to get away, but the girl toppled over and pinned her to the ground. The girl leaned towards Patty. The crablike thing in her hair bent its eye stalks to her. Peering at her with an intention to kill, but not with malice. It was second nature to the crab thing to do what crab things do to keep crab things alive. It hissed victory. The girl's maw moving in unison with the creature's. It was controlling her. The thing was the puppet and the grosser thing was the puppeteer.

The Maw snapped and bit as the two rolled into the sand, fighting for dominance. And life. Patty grunted muffled screams. The girl emanated sounds of the roiling ocean.

Patty clawed at the gills on the girl's neck. She groped for air like a beached porpoise, which only made her fight harder and more manic. The girl managed to get herself on top. Her mouth hellishly large. The bonfire allowed Patty to see each row of teeth spiraling down the gullet of eternity. She even saw the crab creature's lips purse in final desperation.

Patty managed to get her hand into the bonfire. Her flesh molten against the white-hot coals of beach wood. She wrapped her flayed hand around a log and pulled. The bonfire exploded into sparks and cinders.

Then all was black.

Magilla cut off Johnny's warbling voice when he saw the figure walking towards them. They both stood and watched as it made its way across the sand.

"Who is it?" Magilla asked.

"If it's that kooky chickie, I'm out of here, man. She wants to cook for me like I'm her old man or something. Who wants that?"

"Weirdsville. But I don't think it's her. The hair's different. Way high."

The girl emerged from the darkness and flickered in the light of the bonfire. She stood for a moment, then placed her hands tightly on either side of Johnny's cringing face.

"Hey, chickie. I know I said I wouldn't be here, but..."

Patty cut him off with a passionate kiss on the lips. Johnny coughed at the overwhelming taste of ocean salt. She gazed deeply at him with her shimmering green eyes as she probed the back of his mouth with her tongue.

He furrowed his brow at the sharp clacking coming from somewhere deep in her beehive.

"Mate with me," she said.

"Ginchy."

Eye Can't Get No Satisfaction
Staci Layne Wilson

"Looks like the aye's have it," said Iris, laughing. "You're outnumbered, overpowered and outta luck, buddy."

"Okay, okay," said Garity with a whiny moan.

Two couples sat in Iris's living room, counting herself and her new boyfriend, Garity.

Iris got up and changed the channel. *Reflections in a Golden Eye* was about to start.

"I'd still rather see *Hondo*," Garity mumbled.

Iris rolled her eyes and sighed. She stole a sidelong glance at the other woman, Pietra, then turned back to the screen. She squinted, but knew it wouldn't really help.

Her eyes were rotting, and there was nothing she could do about it.

Well, they weren't *her* eyes, technically. They'd belonged to a guy named Brady, and she wouldn't be sorry to see them go. Brady had been colorblind, as many men were. But sometimes beggars couldn't be choosers.

Iris blinked as Liz Taylor's screen persona gazed at herself in a mirror with those violet eyes of hers. Panic seized Iris for a second when one of her eyelids closed and stuck. These peepers were getting rank, and fast. She glanced at Garity. The light from the screen played across his green eyes. Yes, they would look nice with her hair. Iris hadn't gone green for nearly six months.

"This movie is a bummer," Garity grumbled, apparently thinking she was looking to him for his opinion.

"You're just jealous of Marlon Brando," Pietra piped up. "Now be quiet."

Iris knew her friends didn't like Garity much. He was embarrassing her more and more with each passing day, and she was getting tired of his crude comments. They'd been seeing each other for two weeks, and she still hadn't given it up yet. A lot of guys would have moved on after the third sexless date, but Iris was beautiful—and on her way to becoming famous.

At least, she hoped so. Iris was an up-and-coming concert photographer. Her work was really starting to catch on in Ohio, and even though the Buckeye State wasn't exactly a rock & roll hotbed, Iris's dedication to shooting every band that came through town was paying off. The local paper had published her work on the front page twice, and she was finally accumulating enough clips to submit to *Rolling Stone*. But her ultimate goal was to have a galley show with her name as the headliner. It wouldn't be long now.

When she'd sold her soul to Satan (she always giggled to herself at how very Medieval that sounded), she thought he would take care of everything. Well, to be fair, he *was* keeping up his end of the bargain... but he sure was taking his sweet time. Iris almost regretted the deal, but really it was the only thing she could have done.

She snuggled deeper into Garity's warm body, wedging her shoulder into his armpit. His eyes were glazed over with boredom, but she rather liked the onscreen imagery. It was raw and sensual, and the voyeuristic themes reminded her of her own work—somehow, she always managed to capture musicians at their most candid moments. She'd started to assemble her work for an exhibition a couple of years ago, right around the time she was diagnosed with retinal dystrophy, or retinitis pigmentosa as her doctor called it. Whatever it was called, it sucked.

She would never forget that day. Everything happened so fast. At first, she ignored the blurs and auras, but finally she had to see a doctor. She went in, fully expecting she'd have to wear glasses or contact lenses, or some such nuisance. She never thought it could be as serious as anything requiring surgery. But *this*... Inoperable. Incurable. Unbelievable!

When she'd heard those words coming from the doctor's mouth, her world ended right then and there. Photographing the world's greatest musicians had always been her greatest ambition—not many women were in the game, and she wanted to be the best regardless of gender. And, now in the blink of an eye, her dream was murdered by cruel fate.

She drove herself home, crying her eyes out. The tears blurred her sight even worse than it already was, and the tunnel vision she'd been suffering from seemed to narrow twofold. She remembered how she'd stumbled down the stairs leading to the basement, to her studio. Her sanctuary.

The images she'd captured with her natural eye for composition seemed to mock her. Members of The Electric Prunes, Bonzo Dog Doo-Dah Band, Fanny, and Herman's Hermits... all of them seemed to stare directly into her shriveling soul with their flat paper eyes.

The living room was dark, made darker still by the gloomy night depicted on the screen. "This *is* kind of dumb," she whispered to Garity. "Who's gonna believe Brando as a homosexual?"

She ran her hand, conveniently concealed by the inky shadows, across Garity's thigh and into his lap. Her fingers tickled him through the thin cloth of his chinos. He wasn't wearing any underwear, and she could feel his aroused response.

Garity's hips rose slightly, and he whispered in her ear, "Can we take the skin boat to tuna town tonight?"

Iris stifled a guffaw. *Garity. What a way with words!* No wonder she'd held off so long, even though Brady's eyes were laying almost putrid in her sockets. She cursed Satan again. He really was a perverse S.O.B.

When the Dark Lord peeked out from one of her photos all those months ago, she was desperate. She would have agreed to anything. It was bad enough she had to kill people. Not the act of killing itself... that, in her bitterness, she'd come to enjoy... but it wasn't so simple once she was done. Even though she'd sold her immortal soul, her mortal body was still very much in possession of fingerprints, hair, saliva; all manner of nasty evidence. Not to mention the fact that she was becoming well-known in the local music scene. The pigs were idiots, but what would happen if some private eye put together her connection to the victims?

She'd thought about just keeping the donors alive, stashing them somewhere. After all, a person could live without their eyes. But then she would have to feed them and all. And what if one got away? Nah, it could never work. Satan was right: she had to kill them. The clause in her contract that really had her seeing red though, was the one which stipulated she had to be having sex with the eye donor when she plucked her prize. Satan simply told her, "I like to watch." Just her luck, he was a freakin' Peeping Tom.

Well, tonight Old Scratch would get an eyeful.

...

"Finally," Garity said, two hours later. "I thought they'd never leave."

"I've got you all to myself," Iris purred, hugging Garity the moment the front door closed.

"I don't know what's gotten into you," he gasped, "but I'm next." He took her by the hand and started to lead her back to the sofa.

"No," she demurred. "I have a special place I'd like to take you. My secret lair."

"Hmmm." Garity was intrigued. With eyes fastened to her pert bottom as he followed her down the stairs that led to her studio, it was easy for her to see that Garity could hardly stand the anticipation.

He groped for the light, but Iris stayed his hand. "I've got a flashlight," she said teasingly, making the bland statement sound deliciously dirty.

"So do I," Garity said, bringing her hand to his crotch, which was ready to perform like a three-ring circus.

Iris turned, then knelt.

He closed his eyes and seemed to be waiting for her to unzip his pants.

Nothing happened.

When he looked again, he saw Iris had her back to him, held the flashlight in her hand, and was tugging at something on the floor. "What are you doing?"

"Taking you to my lair," Iris replied.

"This isn't it?"

"No, baby. It's *below* the basement. There's a yummy little love chamber down there," she said, lifting a square section from the floor.

She saw the hesitation in his face. She flashed him a peace sign, then lifted her top.

That's all Garity had to see. He would give his eye-teeth to screw her. He followed her once again, just a short drop down through the opening.

The petite, gorgeously furnished boudoir was ablaze with candle light. Some of Iris's photos were taped to the cement walls, but the focal point was the bed. It was round, and encased in an elaborately carved frame of mahogany wood. Owls, kinkajous, and bullfrogs were carved into the wood, forming a circle. Iris flicked an unseen switch, and the bed began to turn slowly.

"I've heard of a revolving door," Garity said with an ear-to-ear grin. "But a revolving bed? This is some next-level Hefner shit, right here!"

"You ain't seen nothing yet," Iris said, slipping out of her clothes. She was aware that he'd been undressing her with his eyes for weeks, but this had to surpass any of his flogging fantasies. While most women her age were burning their bras and letting it all hang out, she liked to be different—below the waist, she wore black leather panties.

"Oh, baby," Garity whistled softly. "You are a sight for sore eyes."

"I have a present for you," Iris said, flushing with pride at his hungry eyes upon her.

"I hope so!" Garity unbuckled his pants and let them drop.

"Ah, ah, ah," she teased him, even going so far as to wag her finger. "I have something for you. Really." She walked over to the nightstand and slid the drawer open.

Garity kicked his pants off and went to her. She was holding a velvet jewelry box out to him. He took it, and eased it open.

"What is it?" he asked, squinting. He frowned.

"It's called a lover's eye." The pin was an antique. "These trinkets were very popular at one time. This one could even be as old as the one King George III's forbidden sweetheart gave to him. She started a fad. She's the one who came up with the idea."

"Putting an eye in a brooch? That's kind of creepy, isn't it?"

"It's supposed to be romantic," Iris explained, letting slip a sigh of exasperation. "You see, when a romance was held secret, a lady couldn't very well give her man the traditional miniature portrait of her whole face. So, she would have just her loving eye painted for him to gaze upon."

"Yeah, okay. It's groovy, I guess."

Goodness gracious, this idiot has about as much artistic appreciation as a parking meter. "Beauty is in the eye of the beholder," Iris said, disappointed but not surprised by Garity's reaction to her gift. Not that he'd be keeping it, anyway.

"Well, I don't know many guys who wear cameos," he said, eyeing the pearls and diamonds that surrounded the painted circle of porcelain. He seemed to be calculating their worth. "But, uh, thanks. Now can I have some of that sweet poontang?"

Iris shook her head. "You are too much, Garity." She took the brooch from him and set it on the nightstand, propped up so the eye could watch them.

She flicked the radio on. Old Blue Eyes was singing about doing it his way. She turned the dial until she found a rock station. Now Lou Reed and the Velvet Underground were singing about pale blue eyes. That was more like it.

Garity lay back on the bedspread, and pulled her on top of him. "Ahhhhh," he sighed. "You feel soooo good."

God. Can't guys think of anything else to say? If only I could take his tongue, too. But Iris had to admit to herself he felt pretty good, too. It had been over a month since she'd had sex. This was only a means to an end, but what the hell. She might as well enjoy it. She rocked harder and faster, while he lay like a stone, letting her do all the work. It didn't take long. A few "Oh, baby's" later, it was all over.

Iris leaned down to kiss Garity—the last kiss he would ever get.

"Ugh! Oh my God! What the fuck!?" He tried to scramble from beneath her, but he couldn't dodge the falling eyeball. His face twisted in horror as it hung off her cheek, the ocular nerve clinging.

Then the gelatinous ball plopped down and landed right in his chest hair, oozing putrid-smelling yellow fluid.

What a fiasco!

Nothing like this had ever happened to her before. Iris knew she had to act fast; she could barely see now. She groped underneath the plump satin pillow and immediately connected with what she was looking for. She locked her legs tighter around Garity's waist as his member slipped from her and the rest of his body tried to follow suit. She had to hold him still as she aimed the dagger for his wildly-pulsing throat. Using one hand, she drove the blade through Garity's windpipe so brutally it ripped through the bedspread and into the mattress.

As he twitched, Iris pulled the dagger free and ducked to avoid the blood geyser. She went right to work, prying his eyes out with the pointed tip. Dead eyes wouldn't do. She had to get them while his heart still beat, no matter how weak the pulse.

She bent her head and gave a shake, coaxing Brady's other rancid eye to drop out, then shoved the fresh new ones in.

It was like a light had been turned on. She sighed in wonder at her renewed sight. Even though the chamber was lit only by candles,

Iris could see the vivid redness of Garity's blood splashed against her white sheets like it was in Technicolor.

Static blared from the radio. Then a distant, dreamy voice began to sing about jeepers and creepers and asking where'd you get those eyes. Such an old chestnut, but then again, the owner of her soul wasn't a very with-it guy.

A tendril of smoke began to writhe from the pupil of the lover's eye brooch. Iris sighed. Such a drama-queen—he always had to make an Entrance, capital E.

The smoke shaped itself into freakish monstrosity for a moment, then he remembered: Iris preferred him in his humanoid form. He'd been named Beelzebub then, and thank God—no wait, thank Eric Clapton—he'd been handsome.

"What's knittin' kitten?" He asked, twisting his chiseled visage into some semblance of a smile, then joined her on the bed. He brushed Garity's corpse aside with a single swipe and it dropped wetly to the floor. "You look swell."

"You're talking 1930s again," Iris reminded him, affectionately brushing his cheek, and tickling his goatee with a bloody hand.

"Sorry," he chuckled. "It's hard to keep up with the language when 500 years is like five minutes."

"Well, I hope you can spare five minutes for me," she said with a wink.

...

The next morning, Iris was feeling antsy. She had a lot of retouching to do, but she couldn't concentrate on her work. Doing something as normal as site-seeing helped to make her feel normal after a night of eye-popping Satanic sex, so she decided to drive to the museum. There was an Art Kane exhibit, and she wanted to see it.

She wandered aimlessly around the gallery for several minutes, but instead of relaxing her, the master rock photographer's images of The Who, Dylan, and Morrison only pestered her envy. When would *her* photographs be on these walls?

Iris decided that she should take a break and have a bite to eat. She made her way to the overpriced café and ordered a Southern dish—rice, with black-eyed beans—and took her meal to the outside dining area.

There was only one seat left, and it was across from a woman about her age. Shyly, she walked over and asked, "Is this seat taken?"

"No. Please," the woman gestured, indicating that Iris should sit.

"Thanks," she said, seating herself on the plastic chair. When she smiled at her impromptu dining companion, she saw that she was already forgotten—the girl was staring past her shoulder as if she wasn't even there. *How rude.*

She forked at her food, lost in thought. If she could pick up a few more gigs, she could afford a Hasselblad—it was the coolest camera, with its ground glass top-down viewfinder placed low. She liked the idea of not having to press her precious eye against the camera.

Minutes passed, but the woman stayed with her even though she'd already finished her meal. Finally, she spoke. "Aren't you hungry?"

"I'm afraid my eyes were bigger than my stomach," Iris said, meeting the woman's eyes. They really were quite astonishing. Light, powder-blue and they had a dreamy, sort of faraway gaze. She'd never seen anything quite like them. "So, what brings you here?"

"The flower gardens," she replied. "I love to smell the Irises."

"Bull's eye! That's my name!"

"Get out," the woman chuckled. "Really? I'm Jordana Winkler." She extended her right hand. "My friends call me Wink."

She grasped the proffered hand, and felt the burns before she saw them. The pink, shiny skin was knotty yet smooth, like an orange peel. "What happened?" she blurted, immediately wishing she could take it back. Now *she* was the rude one.

Wink's brow furrowed. "I grabbed a hot poker." She swallowed nervously. "I don't like to talk about it."

"Oh, I'm sorry! Gosh, I feel so stupid."

"Hey, no harm done." Her hand slipped away. Her blow-torch blue eyes now seemed to bore into Iris's. She was staring quite unabashedly.

"Like what you see?" Iris asked teasingly. "Have an eye for the ladies?" *How about two eyes for this lady?* she added to herself. The more she looked at them, the more she wanted those dreamy baby blues. They are so very beautiful, so perfect. She had to have them.

Iris took Wink by the hand, and the couple headed for the parking lot.

"Want to follow me?" Iris asked, when they arrived at her car.

"I don't drive. Give me a ride?"

I'll give you a ride, alright.

...

Wink was cute, but clingy as hell. Even worse than Garity. She kept groping Iris in the car, almost causing an accident. When she wasn't doing that, she was squeezing her hand, gripping her shoulder, or tugging at her blouse sleeve.

When they got back to her place, Iris poured them large glasses of red wine—hers was for obliteration, and Wink's was to keep her hands on something other than Iris for just a minute or two.

"Let's not pretend, Iris," Wink said, downing her wine in a single swig. "The drink is nice, but we both know why I'm here."

Irish laughed. A smoky, sexy chuckle. She only *thought* she knew why she was here. "Well, then. Let the games begin." She turned, and Wink grabbed for her hand. "I'll take you down to my lair."

"Lair? Kinky!"

"Downstairs," she replied, hurrying. She wanted to just get this over with. She was regretting having brought this handsy girl home, but she really wanted those glorious eyes in her skull ASAP.

"Downstairs?" Wink hesitated.

She guided Wink's hand to the taut curve of her ass, and purred, "I'll make it worth your while."

In her eagerness, Wink stumbled on the first stair but quickly recovered. She lowered herself carefully and cautiously down the hole. Once inside, she showed no reaction to the beautifully appointed chamber boudoir.

"These are some of my photographs," Iris said with a sweeping *ta-da!* gesture. "I'm especially proud of the one of Napoleon the IV."

"Huh?"

Iris pointed at the photo. "You know. He had that hit, *They're Coming to Take Me Away, Ha-Haaa.*"

Wink just shrugged.

Iris was a little disappointed her date didn't compliment her work, let alone even look at it, but by now she'd decided the chick was off her rocker. All the more reason to take her out.

She led Wink to the bedside and told her she wanted to show her something. Iris held the treasure out to her, but Wink didn't even deign to dip her gaze.

"It's a cameo brooch, called a lover's eye."

"Oh. Yes, I've seen them," the unwitting donor replied impatiently, turning away.

"Huh, okay." Iris dutifully propped the eye up on the nightstand, then seated herself on the bed. Wink was still turned away from her. "Are you mad at me? Gonna give me the evil eye now?"

Wink whirled around and grabbed her, hard. "Stop teasing me!" She heaved herself onto Iris, and they hit the floor in a tangle of thrashing arms and legs.

This was no good. The eye couldn't see them on the floor. "Let's move to the bed," Iris suggested.

Wink practically threw her on the mattress, then scrambled up to join her.

Iris glanced over at the lover's eye, which was already beginning to smoke. He was watching. She reached out and felt for the dagger.

Wink was just clambering on top of her when Iris drove the knife into her back. The woman went still.

Iris tore Garity's green eyes out of her head, tossing them aside like old candy-wrappers. She couldn't wait to have Wink's otherworldly blue eyes. Blindly, Iris jerked the dagger free from Wink's spine, then dumped the nearly-dead woman onto her back. Iris took the blade to the woman's orbs with practiced precision.

A split-second before the first one shot across the room and pinged off the cement wall, Iris knew something was terribly wrong. When the blade-tip hit something solid, making a scraping sound, she dropped the knife and ran her hands over Wink's slack face.

Squinting with unseeing disbelief, Iris tapped Wink's intact eye with the end of her fingernail. Glass. She groped for the empty socket, and felt the bumpy orange-peel skin.

Iris caught a whiff of sulfur and heard a faint *poof* as Satan materialized. She fumbled and felt around for Garity's eyes.

She heard a squishing sound, then chewing and smacking. "Delicious," cooed Satan. "Just like one of those fancy pearl onions that make your breath stink. One of my best inventions, if I may say so."

"What have you done?" Iris cried, still groping the bedspread in vain.

"See what happens when you get greedy, Iris? What did you call it? Ah, yes. Your eyes were too big for your stomach."

"You set me up!" she wailed. "I knew she was too good to be true!"

"Not at all," replied Satan. "Though she could have been one of mine. She's got issues. Can't stand the idea of eye-candy being more beautiful than her. I don't know... I don't think you're all that pretty but beauty's in the eye of the beholder, isn't it? Not that she could really see you. She burned her eyes out with a hot poker a few years ago, but it didn't cure her. I'll bet she was thinking about killing you when you beat her to the punch," Satan giggled. "She only pretended to be turned on. Call it a blindman's bluff, if you will."

His raucous laughter echoed off the cement walls and careened in Iris's head until she had to cover her ears. "What do I do now?"

"What do I care? Find another pair... if you can."

"Can't you help me?"

"Oh, no. Couldn't do that." He patted her knee. He bit into Garity's other eye, chomping loudly.

Iris was full-on sobbing now, tendrils of snot dangling from her flaring nostrils. "I thought you loved me!"

"Come now, dear. You're making a spectacle of yourself. I do love you," Satan soothed, reaching down to stroke her matted hair. He began to sing softly, "I only have eyes for you..."

Iris's screams of rage followed him halfway to Hell.

...

Holly was bleary-eyed with boredom. She hoped she'd be moved off tours and be put in the museum's administrative offices soon. Dealing with the public was not her bag.

"This," she said to the small tour crowd that flanked her, "is the modern photography building. Right now, we have an exhibit featuring local shutterbugs. This first image may disturb some of you, so proceed with caution."

It sure disturbed the hell out of her. Holly would never understand why the museum wanted this photograph. "It's a self-portrait," she said, making sure her voice could be heard by all. "Iris Blume. She took this using a self-timer shortly after she went blind. Very sad. As you can see, she had enormous talent."

"Had?" asked a well-dressed man standing at Holly's shoulder.

Holly nodded. "She committed suicide." She left out the part about how the woman had torn her eyes from their sockets, then carved herself up with an antique dagger.

Holly averted her eyes from the horrible image.

Iris was sitting on a bed. She wore a black blindfold, with blood tricking down her cheeks. In her outstretched, upturned hands, she held two perfectly round, astonishingly blue eyes. Instead of signing her name to the photograph, Iris had scrawled the words, "Eye surrender."

She's Got a Ticket to Die
Staci Layne Wilson

Nature's feet throbbed and the sun had reached a point where it beamed directly into her eyes. "How long have we been standing in line?" she complained.

"Two and a half hours," came the immediate reply. Judalon was wearing red corduroys and sat cross-legged on the sidewalk, her back against the stucco outer wall of the Licorice Pizza record store. She was somewhere in the middle of her well-worn, dog-eared paperback of *The Electric Kool-Aid Acid Test.* "Totally worth it for Sly."

Sly and the Family Stone's eclectic mix of funk, soul, rock, and psychedelic free-form jams had catapulted the band to soaring popularity—but Nature still preferred hard-rocking British blues-based bands like The Who, and that hot new group, Led Zeppelin.

They had been to see Sly just a few months ago. Tickets were almost $9, which was half of her week's pay working part-time at the Orange Julius, so Nature felt like she was good on seeing that band for a while. She'd much rather check out a show she hadn't seen yet. But her friend didn't want to go alone—she said she needed a wing-woman just in case they got backstage.

That was Judalon's thing. But Nature had to admit it was fun getting all dolled up and sweet-talking the roadies into giving them backstage passes. That wasn't necessary at the clubs, of course, but the bigger acts played forums and halls that had pretty tight security.

Nature hadn't brought a book with her, so she strained to hear what was playing from inside the record-store—it sounded like a news bulletin—and let her mind wander. She looped a frazzled end of her long, light brown hair around her index finger and twisted it, 'round and 'round. She'd definitely iron away her curls before the concert, and maybe she'd wear her new mini-dress with her super-groovy bright-yellow go-go boots. Her current sore feet protested the future pain, and she rethought her outfit. Ironed hair for sure, and moccasins that would go good with jeans and a halter-top.

She glanced down at Judalon, who was engrossed in her book. She was better-looking than Nature, and she was better-developed, too. She'd probably wear an attention-grabbing Mary Quant minidress and Courreges Couture boots to the concert, and would have no problem getting backstage. A rich bitch like her certainly didn't need a wing-woman, but, Nature thought, being "the pretty friend" made for good contrast and helped Judalon stand out.

Perhaps to torture herself, Nature asked, "What are you wearing to the concert?"

Judalon's green eyes sparkled in the sun, striking even from behind her oversized Italian Vogue sunglasses. "Ooh, I have the cutest new dress. I got it on Carnaby Street last month. I haven't shown it to you? It's skintight, low-cut, and super-short! Sly is going to love it," she grinned.

"Sounds a little slutty." She was all for free love, but not free sex.

"I'd rather be looked over than overlooked." Judalon fake-primped her hair and winked lasciviously. "Mae West said that. Words to live by."

"Yeah," Nature said agreeably. She was working on not being judgmental, which was a hard habit to break considering the card-carrying NRA member, Nixon-loving fascists who'd raised her.

Nature felt a friendly hand on her shoulder. "Hey, Nan." It was Jerry, the guy from her third-period Social Studies class.

"*Nature*, please," she corrected him. "Nan is my slave-name."

"Right. Sorry." Jerry's shaggy mop bounced in time with his nodding head. His eyelashes were blonde and a weak mustache embroidered his upper lip, but Nature thought he was kind of cute.

"And remember," snapped Judalon as she scooched her rear one more spot up in line, "I'm Jude. As in, *Hey Jude.*"

Jerry moved with the slow-shuffling crowd. "Well, then, I guess that makes me Garcia."

Judalon shot him a venomous stare. "Hardly," she retorted.

"Jeez," Jerry muttered to Nature. "Who's on the rag?"

Nature gave him a look.

"Don't tell me the rabbit died," Jerry went on, oblivious.

"That is just cruel," said Nature. Not about the remark, but about the pregnancy test procedure.

Jerry laughed. "You really believe that? That's not how it's done."

"Whatever," Nature said, feeling stupid. Science wasn't her strong suit. She changed the subject. "Are you here for Sly and the Family Stone tickets? Because if you are, you're cutting the line."

"No, I'm here to get a few copies Unknown Assailant's album before they're all gone."

"Why would they be gone?" Nature asked.

Unknown Assailant was her favorite new band. The band of Brits had come onto the scene a few months before and hadn't toured in America yet, but she knew they were going to be big. Maybe even bigger than The Beatles. Their debut album *Hostile Witness* had soared straight to the #1 slot on the Billboard charts thanks to their toe-tapping poppy hooks. While the songs sounded buoyant and hopeful, their lyrics were dark and disturbing. They sang about homicide, genocide, suicide, infanticide, and even pesticide. Nature played the LP on her hi-fi repeatedly, so much so that her parents worried about her "obsession." Ridiculous.

Her parents were so square—they lived their lives with blinders on, blissfully ignoring the suffering that was going on every day. Whenever the news showed footage from Vietnam, had a report about police brutality, or talked about a yippee protest march, one of them would inevitably get up and change the channel. Their old-ass generation ignored or discounted facts that didn't fit into their happy little bubble. Whenever Nature tried to open "Ward and June's" eyes to the real world, they said she was a child and she just didn't understand yet how it all works. Then they used their favorite statistics like a drunk uses lamp posts: for support rather than illumination. They chose to live in a land of mirrors, shadows, and echoes—the perfect nuclear family. It made Nature want to puke.

She felt even sicker when Jerry answered her question.

"Because the whole band died. Haven't you heard?"

"What?" said several nearby teeny-boppers, their voices rising in unison.

"What?" Nature repeated.

Jerry stood up a little straighter, as if proud to be the bearer of such momentous news. He spoke with Socratic intensity as he relayed the story. "It's true. I heard it on the radio. They all drowned." He paused for effect. "They were given brand-new MGB Roadsters by their record company for going platinum, so the boys decided to drive them around Trafalgar Square. Then they started racing each other. They turned the park into a regular Grand Prix, circling the fountain faster and faster, until somehow, they all crashed into each other and wound up in the water. That's where they drowned."

"Oh, my God," Nature cried. "They're dead? All of them?"

"Um, excuse me," said Judalon, standing to face Jerry. "That's bullshit. I've been to Trafalgar Square, and I've thrown coins into that very fountain. It's only a foot deep. And who's gonna drown in a convertible? Nobody's that dumb."

Jerry shrugged. "Unknown Assailant was, apparently. Four times over."

Nature's brain spun. How could it be? Lead singer Alfred Tomlinson: dead. Guitarist Allen Payne: dead. Bassist Dixon Yates: dead. Drummer Oliver "Octopus" Gibson: dead. So young, so talented. It wasn't fair! She felt her eyes sting with the threat of tears. She heard the chatter of her fellow music lovers, but she couldn't focus on anything they were saying. All she could comprehend was her own shock and devastation.

Judalon nudged Nature. "Hold my place in line. I'm gonna go inside the store to ask if it's true." She gave Jerry side-eye. "Not that I don't believe you, but... I don't believe you." She made her way to the head of the ticket line and into the store.

"They were my favorite band," Nature told Jerry.

"They were cool," Jerry agreed, eyes downcast. "Sorry, I didn't mean to bum you out."

They stood in uncomfortable silence for a few minutes before Judalon returned.

"Man, I really was hoping to ball one of them," lamented the groupie.

So, it was true. Unknown Assailant was yet another rock & roll statistic. Judalon said reports confirmed they were high on windowpane acid, magic mushrooms, and banana peels. Nature could imagine the antidrug lecture she'd be getting from her parents when they found out how her favorite band had kicked it.

"Weren't they supposed to be touring here soon?" Judalon asked. Her question was directed to the Unknown Assailant expert, Nature.

Nature pulled herself together. "Yeah, but no dates were announced." She blinked back tears. "I can't believe they're gone. I'd give anything to bring them back." She flicked her gaze to Jerry and muttered, "You'd better get in there and buy those records."

Jerry put his hand on Nature's shoulder in an awkward attempt to comfort her, then he turned and made his way to the record store's entrance.

"Let's go," said Judalon. "I got our tickets." She held them up and waved them in the air.

Nature blinked through her haze of sorrow. "How?" She glanced at the long line still ahead of them.

"I have my ways," she smirked, giving her low-cut top a tug, showing off her ample bosoms. Her expression turned serious. "And the tickets are on me." She held one out to Nature.

"Thanks, Jude." She listlessly took the ticket, then pocketed it. "I think I'm gonna go home now." She sniffled, tasting salty tears at the back of her throat.

Her friend shrugged. "Okay, that's groovy. See you in class tomorrow."

Nature lived only a few blocks from the Licorice Pizza, but she shuffled down Long Beach Boulevard so slowly that it took her the better part of an hour. The world felt out of whack, silent without the music of Unknown Assailant, yet she was bombarded with ugly sounds—cars whooshed by like cannonballs, and the panhandlers begging for a handout had voices like bursts of radio static. Finally, she reached her front door. She let herself in with her key, then made a beeline for the sanctuary of her bedroom. She almost made it.

"Nan," called her dad, unseen from another room. "Come here."

She obeyed, standing in the doorway of the den. "Ward" was sitting in his ancient easy chair, and "June" was on the plastic-protected floral sofa, knitting. She looked at them with an eyebrow raised in petulance.

"You got a phone call," said Dad. "A boy. You know you're not allowed to date yet, Nan."

"Okay?" her voice rose in question. She hadn't given her phone number to any boy, so she couldn't imagine who it was. "Was it Jerry?"

"Who's Jerry?" Dad asked, pronouncing the name with disdain. "Some rebel without a job?"

"Yeah," Mom chimed in. "Some dummy, dolt, ditz, ding-dong, dunderhead, or dingus?" Mom, a foiled English teacher, spoke using annoying alliteration whenever possible.

Nature stayed silent, knowing that passive-aggressive behavior annoyed her parents like nothing else.

Finally, Dad spoke. "It was *not* Jerry," he said, "and just how many boys are you seeing behind our backs, young lady? It was someone named Alfred. He had a British accent—just how many countries are you trying to date, young lady?—and he said he'd be seeing you soon. Well, I told him he will *not*, that you are only a child, then he laughed and hung up! The nerve!"

"We won't welcome willfulness," Mom said, gnashing her knitting needles together as if they were teeth.

"Sorry," Nature mumbled, "May I be excused?"

Dad waved his arm in dismissal, and went back to reading his newspaper.

She stopped into the kitchen to grab a packet of Ding Dongs—Mom's insult had made her crave something sweet—then went to her room, shutting the door behind her.

It was messy, as usual. While her parents were strict, they did let her slide when it came to her bedroom. It was decorated as she pleased, and she only had to clean it once a month. The green shag carpet matched the avocado curtains, and her bedspread was bright pink. She had a few books on her shelves; mostly holdovers from childhood, which included titles like *Nancy Drew and the Mystery of the Moss-Covered Mansion* (a gift from Mom, of course). She had a desk at which to do her homework, and perched next to that was her hi-fi stereo. *Hostile Witness* was already on the turntable, and she stared at the LP for a moment before turning on the stereo. She watched as the needle dropped at the beginning.

Tearing the wrapping from her Ding Dongs, Nature thought, *This is the first time I'm listening to Unknown Assailant, A.D. After Death.* She wondered if the story of their noble demise would be on the news tonight. Probably not… squares like Walter Cronkite wouldn't know a truly great rock band from their own wrinkly asses.

The first track, *Blofeld's Cat*, went into the hook. "The bald man's pussy's got claws," sang Alfred Tomlinson in his reedy falsetto. Nature let her sad flag fly. She sobbed all the way through *Euphoric Hysterectomy*, *All the*

Disapproving Hereford Cows, and *Bangers and Mash with Spotted Dick*.

After finishing her second Ding Dong, Nature crumpled the wrapper and tossed it to the floor. Then she kicked it under the bed, where it joined other discarded items from the last few weeks.

She stared at her posters of Unknown Assailant—all two of them. As with any new band, their merch would have increased with the rise of their fanbase. These would be collector's items, now. The first poster was standard-issue rock-band cliché: the four members standing in a row, the image distorted by a fisheye lens and the photographer's Dutch tilt. It was the other poster she loved the most, and had her lip-prints on it as proof.

It had Alfred Tomlinson as its focal point, with Allen, Dixon, and Octopus out-of-focus and smaller in the background. Alfred seemed to be looking right at the viewer with his intense, black-and-white eyes. His eyes were not actually black-and-white, of course, but the image was. With so few photos to drool over, and cheap paper being what it was, Nature had decided his eyes must be green. In this particular picture, Alfred's long, wild hair was gathered up in a topknot, his unibrow was sitting low in obvious consternation, and he was sticking his tongue out.

So sexy, so dead. So unfair!

She glanced over at her Halloween costume, which hung on a peg from the inside of the open closet door. All the snobs at Jude's party had snickered behind her back because it was homemade—she just knew it. The thought of her wealthy friend reminded her about the Sly and the Family Stone concert ticket. She'd better put it away before forgetting it and her jeans winding up in the washing machine.

Nature turned the record over and started track one of side two. Then she reached into her pocket and extracted the ticket. She went to her desk and opened the drawer. As she set the ticket down, it curled up and gave her a nasty papercut. "Ouch!" she complained, bringing her stinging finger to her mouth.

She shot the slightly bloody ticket an angry glare, then she saw that it was not for admission to the Sly and the Family Stone concert at all. She narrowed her gaze, bringing the words into focus.

Unknown Assailant
November 1, 1969
Long Beach Arena
VIP Section

"What...?" Nature breathed.

She was alarmed both by the text on the ticket, and the scratchy song playing through her small but serviceable speakers. A tune that wasn't on *Hostile Witness*... before now. It was an old blues standard. She recognized it because they'd just covered the genre in Music Appreciation class. It was called *Ain't No Grave (Gonna Hold This Body Down)*, and while there were a few versions, Sister Rosetta Tharpe's seemed to be everyone's favorite. Only this wasn't Sister Rosetta singing... it was the unmistakable, off-key caterwaul of Alfred Tomlinson.

Her heart thumped in her chest like a moth beating its wings against a white-hot porch light. She began to sweat, and her stomach threatened to eject both Ding Dongs.

Something's not right here. Did Jerry slip me some acid? No, he hadn't given her anything to eat or drink. Jude had handed her the bogus ticket—maybe it was laced with some topical hallucinogen.

She stopped the record, then left her room quietly, closing the door carefully behind her.

She tiptoed to the kitchen, where the telephone was kept. With the slow, precise movements that would make a bomb defuser envious, she took the receiver from its cradle and dialed Jude's number. She didn't have to look it up, because she'd known it by heart ever since they met at a stupid sock hop in the school gym two years before. The line rang a few times, then the maid answered. Thankfully, her friend was home and she came to the phone within seconds—which were like mini-eternities to Nature, who'd be grounded if her parents caught her on the phone before her homework was done.

"Jude," she whispered, her lips so close to the microphone that they touched the handset.

"WHAT?! I CAN'T HEAR YOU," shouted Jude so loudly that she was sure "Ward and June" would hear from the den.

"Shhh. I saw the ticket. How did you do that?"

"DO WHAT?!"

"Shhh. How did you change the ticket from Sly and the Family Stone to Unknown Assailant? It's not funny. You know how much I loved them. That's just cruel, because you know I'll never get real tickets."

"HUH?!"

"Shhh. I mean it. I'm not mad. But why did you do it? Or am I tripping? Did you give me LSD?"

"I have no idea what you're talking about. But it does seem like you're tripping. Go lie down, Nan."

"Nature."

"Okay, fine. Go lie down, Nature, sleep it off, and I'll see you at school tomorrow."

Click.

Jude had hung up on her.

Replacing the receiver to its cradle, she walked in soundless slow-motion back to her room. She opened the door and stepped in. The lights were off. *That's weird*, she thought, *I didn't turn them off.* Then she realized she'd taken a wrong turn and gone into the hall bathroom.

She flicked the switch, entered, and found herself standing outside. She was in a massive, empty parking lot and before her in the distance was the huge, round Long Beach Arena. She turned, grabbing for the doorknob, but it was gone.

She shook her head, and blinked. She'd only tripped on acid once before, and it hadn't been anything like this. She was inside the arena now, seated front-row-center. Dream tickets. Only, this was some kind of nightmare. She tried to stand but found that she was glued to the seat. The stage was empty. She looked left and right, then over her shoulder. She was an audience of one.

The house lights went down, and she heard a band shuffling onto the stage. Four spotlights shone down and Nature watched as four crushed convertible sports cars drove to them, then stopped. Octopus Gibson, both of his arms broken and mangled, was at the drummer's usual spot in back. Dixon Yates, his straggly-haired head lolling to one side, was positioned at stage left. To the right was Allen Payne, who seemed, appropriately enough, to be in great pain from the gaping wound where his chest had once been. The star of the show, front-man Alfred Tomlinson, looked unharmed, albeit soaking wet from his recent drowning.

She peered up at the singer. Despite her abject terror, she also felt the same excitement she might have, had this been a regular concert. She looked into Alfred's eyes, which were not green, but a demonic red, and sighed. Then she began to clap.

The adulation spurred the band to launch into their opening number. They didn't have instruments, so they played the song on their car radios. "The bald man's pussy's got claws," Alfred screeched. Brackish water oozed from his mouth and sputtered onto Nature, who was still fastened to her seat. She basked in it, as if it were his living sweat. The song ended and she applauded again.

"Thank you," said Alfred, his accented voice sounding as if it were coming through a microphone. "It's great to be here in beautiful downtown Long Beach, California. It's great to be anywhere." He looked over his shoulder at his band. "Right, boys? We are dead, after all." He cast his crimson gaze across the stadium of empty chairs, then looked directly at Nature.

His car rolled slowly forward until it reached the edge of the stage. Alfred spoke in a high but menacing voice that sounded like feedback. "It's the Day of the Dead. Do you know what that means?"

She shook her head.

"I heard what you said," Alfred went on, leaning forward in his crumpled seat and peering through the shattered windshield. "You said you'd do anything to bring me back. The Day of the Dead makes that possible."

Before she could ask how, a horn honked.

It was coming from Octopus's mangled MG. "Um, no, mate," said the drummer. "She said she'd give anything to bring us back. Not just *you*, you stuck-up prat!"

"Yeah, that's right," Dixon piled on. "*Us!*"

Alfred turned in his seat. "Shut-up, you lot! Nobody cares about drummers and bass players."

"What about me?" asked Allen, petulance in his voice, which was barely audible thanks to the sucking wound in his chest. "Guitarists are better than singers!"

"Says you!" snapped Alfred, spewing water. "Besides, this fan only has one life to give. I'm claiming it!"

"Then why did you drag us here with you?" Octopus asked, trying unsuccessfully to cross his jangly arms. "I was perfectly happy in the morgue. It was very relaxing."

"You idiot," sneered the lead singer. "That was your body. Your soul is in purgatory." He paused. "Well, it will be until the Almighty decides what to do with you." He turned his attention back to Nature. "Are you ready to die?"

The girl smiled and nodded. "Yes."

Alfred was clearly taken aback. "You are?" He peered at her suspiciously. "What kind of trick is this?"

"No trick," she said. "It's a *trip*. I'm having a bad acid trip. This isn't real, so I'm just going with the flow."

Alfred opened his car door, having to push it hard with his hip to free the latch from its collapsed housing. Water gushed out, flooding the stage floor. "That's annoying," Alfred remarked. "I'll be glad to be back in a dry body."

Nature watched as Octopus exited his own vehicle and rushed to the front of the stage, his arms flopping bonelessly at his sides. "No, you don't!" he shouted. "We are a band. We don't make any decisions without a majority vote. I say I should be the one brought back to life because... because..."

"You can't think of anything, can you?" Allen said, cocking one side of his unibrow. Then he crossed his unbroken arms, taunting the damaged drummer.

All the band members were now standing at the lip of the stage, arguing. Then a fight broke out. Nature saw a flurry of flying fists, furious feet, and—Mom would be proud—facinorous faces, then the scuffle stopped as abruptly as it had started.

Allen, who'd always come off as the most diplomatic in the interviews Nature had read, took a few limping steps to the edge of the stage. He smiled at her. His teeth had been broken in the pile-up and hung in jagged shards from his pale gums. "Let's ask the fan who she wants to bring back."

"Whom," Dixon corrected.

"Since when are you professor of grammar?" Alfred said, then harumphed. He stomped over to Allen's side. He looked down at Nature, then snapped his fingers. "I'm your favorite, aren't I?" he asked her.

Nature felt the seat loosen beneath her. She stood up. She was lightheaded but otherwise okay. "Yes, you are."

"That's what you think," said Octopus. "I'm the one who wrote your favorite song. Yes, that's right. Even though we all got equal credit on the album, it was me who came up with *Baby Formula*. I wrote it when I was in my first band."

Nature considered this. Given the 15-minute drum solo lead-in to the tune, it made sense. But still... she was in love with Alfred Tomlinson. Then she started to think about the logistics. If she were to give her life for the singer's, then she'd be dead and he'd be alive. That wouldn't work out very well in terms of them being boyfriend and girlfriend. Then again, if this was all some kind of drug-induced fugue, she had nothing to lose.

"We don't have all night," prompted Alfred. "The Day of the Dead lasts only 24-hours, you know."

"Right," she said, climbing up to join the band. She got to her feet, careful of the slippery puddles, then looked out into the empty stadium. Even without people there, it was a rush to be on stage in a vast auditorium. "I just have a few questions. If I give my life for you—any one of you—what happens to me? Am I just dead and gone, or will there still be something of my consciousness living on in you?"

"Hmm," grunted Dixon with admiration. "She's pretty deep for a groupie."

"Look," Alfred barked, taking Nature by the elbow. "I don't know. But just a minute ago, you were all gung-ho about sacrificing your life for me. As I said, there's an expiration date. Now, I don't want to have to force you, but," his eyes turned even redder, then glowed with infernal flame, "I will if I must. And it will be very painful."

She didn't want pain, even if she couldn't be sure whether this was all in her imagination. "Okay," she said, "How do we do this?"

Alfred grinned, then shot his band members a look of triumph. "Ha! I knew she'd pick me!" He squeezed her elbow. "Thank you, my little bird. So, here's how it works—" While still in midsentence, Alfred yanked Nature's mouth open, pulling her jaw down so forcefully, the bone cracked. Then he brought his mouth to hers.

Through the throbbing agony, she felt water in her mouth, then in her throat. She coughed and sputtered, twisting her head. But it was no use. Alfred was filling her with Trafalgar Square fountain water and there was nothing she could do about it. She realized, with awful clarity, that this was all too real and she really was dying. To scream for help would flood her already-exhausted lungs more quickly, so she cut her cry short and stayed quiet. She had to do something.

Then a thought came to her, as if sent from a higher power: California is nine hours behind London. She couldn't be sure exactly of the time at that precise moment, but it could very well be November 2 in the UK, which is where Alfred's body was. Did that make a difference? Knowing that she was running out of time regardless, Nature raised her knee and drove the bony nub as hard as she could up and into Alfred's gonads.

"Ugh!" he stumbled back, grabbing his crotch.

Nature bent over and vomited. A waterfall of H20 was ejected, and it kept on coming. It was like Hoover Dam had broken—it was far more water than she'd taken on. Her ears rang and her eyes went blind with the effort it took to expel whatever evil Alfred had put into her. Her knees buckled and she fell to the stage floor. She blinked against unconsciousness and saw Alfred fighting the tide, trying desperately to stay above water.

He was drowning all over again.

...

Nature knew she was lying down, but she wasn't sure where she was. Her broken jaw pulsated dully, her lungs ached with each shallow breath, and her throat felt like she'd tried to swallow a cheese-grater. After taking mental stock, she opened her eyes. Everything was white. Her parents were there, looking down at her with concern, and Judalon was sitting on a chair at the far end of the room. *Did these three give their souls for the remaining three Unknown Assailant band members? Are we all in purgatory?* Then smells and sounds came into play and her mind cleared. *I'm in the hospital. I'm alive.*

Unable to speak, she made a small whimper.

Her mother's hands found hers. "Oh, honey." She glanced at her husband. "Her eyes are open." Then back to her daughter. "Nan, how are you feeling?"

Nature tried to form words to ask what happened and why Mom wasn't speaking in her usual annoying alliteration, but she could only sputter.

Jude got up and joined Nature's parents.

"Should we tell her?" Mom asked, addressing no one in particular.

"Why don't you let me?" Judalon suggested, gently. "Want to go get a coffee or something?"

Demonstrating unusual understanding, "Ward and June" agreed and left the room, shutting the door behind them.

"Do you like the room?" she asked, seating herself on the edge of the hospital bed. "It's private. Daddy pulled some strings." Jude's dad was, no doubt, a major donor to charities and hospitals. "You're on suicide watch," she announced. She never was one to mince words.

Nature raised her eyebrows in question.

"Yeah," she went on. "You tried to drown yourself in the bathtub, which is almost as dumb as Alfred Tomlinson dying in two feet of water," she said with a wry, not unwarranted smile. "Somehow you slipped and broke your jaw."

Nature grunted. No wonder she couldn't talk.

Jude patted her hand. "I know what it means to be a fan. But you don't have to take it so hard. These things happen. Maybe Alfred was trying to be more like his own idol, Brian Jones. And least, that's what the rest of the guys are saying. But that doesn't mean *you* have to make such a dramatic statement." She sighed. "Don't do that again. Who would be my concert buddy if you were gone, huh?"

Great, Nature thought. *I came back from the brink of death only to be your wing-woman.* Then she caught it. She realized that only Alfred's death had been spoken of. "Ah-red?" she managed, feeling a trickle of drool at the corner of her mouth.

Her friend either didn't understand, or chose to ignore the question. "I have a surprise for you." She smiled impishly. "I got a message to Unknown Assailant's manager.

Daddy's known Sid for years, and, well—Allen, Dixon, and Oliver are here to wish their biggest fan a speedy recovery!"

Nature wriggled into a semi-sitting position. Her heart pounded and her throat constricted. *This isn't right.*

"I'll go get them!" Jude said.

Nature grabbed for her arm, but it was too late. Judalon was already at the door.

The moment it opened, the band hustled inside and went directly to the bedside.

She cringed. Their dripping, broken bodies and awful, mangled faces flashed in her memory. She stared at the three young, handsome faces before her, each of them smiling awkwardly. They were fine. Not a scratch on any of them. They hadn't died. Only Alfred was gone.

"Hey, Nan," said Octopus, waving. "We're here to make you feel better."

Nature was vaguely aware of Judalon in the background, and her parents coming into the room, but they seemed blurry and far away. The room warped and shifted—a hospital one second, a concert stage the next.

"We are so grateful to meet our biggest fan," Allen said, smiling, "but we can't stay for long."

"We have Alfred's funeral to attend." Dixon leaned in, then whispered, "Thank you for sacrificing him."

We hope you enjoyed *Rock & Roll Nightmares: Along Comes Scary*, the '60s edition. If you did, please kindly leave a review, and be on the lookout for the other books in this series.

Author Bios

Staci Layne Wilson is an L.A. native who enjoys traffic, wildfires, and earthquakes—but since her recent move to Las Vegas, she's learned to love 110-degree summers, drive-thru wedding chapels, and casinos that still reek of the Rat Pack's cigars. The best day of Staci's life was when she got to interview Jack White and Jimmy Page on the red carpet for *It Might Get Loud*. She has directed a music documentary— *The Ventures: Stars on Guitars*, about her dad's band—and her next film, cowritten with Darren Gordon Smith, is *The Second Age of Aquarius*, a sci-fi rock & roll rom-com. Catch up with Staci at: www.stacilaynewilson.com

Jeff Strand is the Bram Stoker Award- nominated author of over 50 books, including *Pressure*, *Dweller*, and *Clowns vs. Spiders*. He's seen "Weird Al" Yankovic in concert on every tour since 1996, and wishes he'd seen The Arrogant Worms on all their tours but they don't often leave Canada. He's never met Alice Cooper but he's sure the guy would be super cool. You can visit Jeff's website at www.jeffstrand.com

Marco Mannone is an L.A.-based horror screenwriter and 2019 BloodList alumni. In-between screenplays, Marco has also worked as a freelance journalist, which is how he came to interview The Doors (his all-time favorite band) for their documentary *When You're Strange*. Unfortunately, Jim was not available. Find Marco on Twitter @MarcoMannone and Instagram @marco_macabre

Renee Mallett has made a career out of spending the night in haunted hotels and living to tell the tale. When not writing books about New England's spookiest places she can usually be found in creepy old textile mills, behind the counter at Pop Cultured (her indie comic and gaming shop), or making art at Nova Art Studios. Formerly the art director for a music magazine, her kids say her singing voice could raise the dead and to stick to art and writing, please. You can visit her online at www.ReneeMallett.com

Shane Bitterling is an award-winning screenwriter with over thirty produced movies under his Devo energy dome. A few that he'll admit to are *Reel Evil*, *Beneath Loch Ness* and the award-winning *Weedjies*, as well as *Witchfinder*, which is in eternal development hell at 20th Century Fox. His published work can be found in the anthologies *Hell Comes to Hollywood*, *18 Wheels of Horror*, and others. His (not just for) children's book, *The Year Without Halloween*, might be your favorite thing. The

Monkees are his Beatles, and he still watches Hee-Haw every Sunday. Keep up via Twitter @ShaneBitterling

Darren Gordon Smith is a filmmaker, writer, and musician. He is the co-creator of *Repo! The Genetic Opera*, which is considered by *Rolling Stone* magazine to be one of the top 25 cult films of all time and stars Anthony Head, Sarah Brightman, and Ogre of Skinny Puppy. Darren plays a mean keytar.

Audiobook Narrator

Jennifer Knighton is an L.A.-based actor and writer. She's found a niche in horror that she never expected to find. Music has always been a major influence in her life (rumor has it, *Desperado* is the song that made her dad decide to propose to her mom). She's been singing with an a capella pirate group called Marooned since the late '90s. Follow via Facebook @jennifer.knighton.9

Special thanks—Aaron Kai, Lisa Johnson Mandell, James Mandell, Lotti Pharriss-Knowles, Oriel Collins, and last but far from least, Linda Rose.

Manufactured by Amazon.ca
Bolton, ON